Stories of Space

Stories of Space

Edited by Betty M. Owen

SCHOLASTIC BOOK SERVICES
New York Toronto London Auckland Sydney Tokyo

Grateful acknowledgment is made to the following authors and publishers for the use of copyrighted materials. Every effort has been made to obtain permission to use previously published material. Any errors or omissions are unintentional.

Robert Abernathy for his story, "The Rotifers," copyright 1953 by Quinn Publishing Company, Inc.

Peg Campbell for "Who Goes There?" by John W. Campbell, copyright © 1938 by Street & Smith Publications, Inc.; copyright renewed © 1966 by The Conde Nast Publications, Inc.

Doubleday & Company, Inc. for "Does a Bee Care?" from BUY JUPITER by Isaac Asimov, copyright © 1957 by Quinn Publishing Company.

Henry Gregor Felsen for his story, "The Spaceman Cometh," copyright © 1955 by *Collier's Magazine.*

Victor Gollancz, Ltd. for British Commonwealth rights to "Does A Bee Care?" by Isaac Asimov.

Hugh Hood for his story, "After the Sirens," copyright © 1960 by *Esquire Magazine.*

Scott Meredith Literary Agency, Inc., 845 Third Avenue, New York, NY 10022 for "The Haunted Space Suit," by Arthur C. Clarke, copyright © 1963 by United Newspapers Magazine Corporation; "The Nine Billion Names of God" by Arthur C. Clarke, copyright 1953 by Ballantine Books, Inc., copyright © 1967 by Arthur C. Clarke; "Collecting Team" by Robert Silverberg, copyright © 1957 by Headline Publications.

Clifford D. Simak for his story, "Condition of Employment," copyright © 1960 by Galaxy Publishing Corporation, for *Galaxy Magazine,* April 1960.

ISBN 0-590-31264-2

12 11 10 9 8 7 6 5 4 3 2 1   12   9/7 0 1 2 3 4/8

Printed in the U.S.A.   06

CONTENTS

Who Goes There?

JOHN W. CAMPBELL

The thing had lain under the Antarctic ice
for millions of years, imprisoned within
the frozen hull of a ship. Now it lay inside the camp, its hideous features en-
cased in ice, mercifully hidden by a tarp.
As the ice slowly melted, a faint, dis-
agreeable odor of something alive, yet
alien, floated through the darkness, con-
taminating the air. A clue the survivors
would later recall as the beginning of
their nightmare.

The place stank. A queer, mingled stench
that only the ice-buried cabins of an Antarctic
camp know, compounded of reeking human
sweat, and the heavy, fish-oil stench of melted
seal blubber. An overtone of liniment com-
batted the musty smell of sweat-and-snow-
drenched furs. The acrid odor of burnt cooking
fat, and the animal, not-unpleasant smell of
dogs, diluted by time, hung in the air.

Lingering odors of machine oil contrasted sharply with the taint of harness dressing and leather. Yet, somehow, through all that reek of human beings and their associates — dogs, machines, and cooking — came another taint. It was a queer, neck-ruffling thing, a faintest suggestion of an odor alien among the smells of industry and life. And it was a life-smell. But it came from the thing that lay bound with cord and tarpaulin on the table, dripping slowly, methodically onto the heavy planks, dank and gaunt under the unshielded glare of the electric light.

Blair, the little bald-pated biologist of the expedition, twitched nervously at the wrappings, exposing clear, dark ice beneath and then pulling the tarpaulin back into place restlessly. His little birdlike motions of suppressed eagerness danced his shadow across the fringe of dingy gray underwear hanging from the low ceiling, the equatorial fringe of stiff, graying hair around his naked skull a comical halo about the shadow's head.

Commander Garry brushed aside the lax legs of a suit of underwear, and stepped toward the table. Slowly his eyes traced around the rings of men sardined into the Administration Building. His tall, stiff body straightened finally, and he nodded. "Thirty-seven. All here." His voice was low, yet carried the clear authority of the commander by nature, as well as by title.

"You know the outline of the story back of that find of the Secondary Pole Expedition. I have been conferring with Second-in-Command McReady, and Norris, as well as Blair and Dr. Copper. There is a difference of opinion, and because it involves the entire group, it is only just that the entire Expedition personnel act on it.

"I am going to ask McReady to give you the details of the story, because each of you has been too busy with his own work to follow closely the endeavors of the others. McReady?"

Moving from the smoke-blued background, McReady was a figure from some forgotten myth, a looming, bronze statue that held life, and walked. Six feet four inches he stood as he halted beside the table, and with a characteristic glance upward to assure himself of room under the low ceiling beams, straightened. His rough, clashingly orange windproof jacket he still had on, yet on his huge frame it did not seem misplaced. Even here, four feet beneath the drift-wind that droned across the Antarctic waste above the ceiling, the cold of the frozen continent leaked in, and gave meaning to the harshness of the man. And he was bronze — his great red-bronze beard, the heavy hair that matched it. The gnarled, corded hands gripping, relaxing, gripping, and relaxing on the table planks were bronze. Even the deep-sunken eyes beneath heavy brows were bronzed.

Age-resisting endurance of the metal spoke in the cragged heavy outlines of his face, and the mellow tones of the heavy voice. "Norris and Blair agree on one thing; that animal we found was not — terrestrial in origin. Norris fears there may be danger in that; Blair says there is none.

"But I'll go back to how, and why we found it. To all that was known before we came here, it appeared that this point was exactly over the South Magnetic Pole of Earth. The compass does point straight down here, as you all know. The more delicate instruments of the physicists, instruments especially designed for this expedition and its study of the magnetic pole, detected a secondary effect, a secondary, less powerful magnetic influence about eighty miles southwest of here.

"The Secondary Magnetic Expedition went out to investigate it. There is no need for details. We found it, but it was not the huge meteorite or magnetic mountain Norris had expected to find. Iron ore is magnetic, of course; iron more so — and certain special steels even more magnetic. From the surface indications, the secondary pole we found was small, so small that the magnetic effect it had was preposterous. No magnetic material conceivable could have that effect. Soundings through the ice indicated it was within one hundred feet of the glacier surface.

"I think you should know the structure of the place. There is a broad plateau, a level sweep that runs more than 150 miles due south from the Secondary Station, Van Wall says. He didn't have time or fuel to fly farther, but it was running smoothly due south then.

Right there, where that buried thing was, there is an ice-drowned mountain ridge, a granite wall of unshakable strength that has dammed back the ice creeping from the south.

"And four hundred miles due south is the South Polar Plateau. You have asked me at various times why it gets warmer here when the wind rises, and most of you know. As a meteorologist I'd have staked my word that no wind could blow at −70 degrees, that no more than a five-mile wind could blow at −50, without causing warming due to friction with ground, snow and ice and the air itself.

"We camped there on the lip of that ice-drowned mountain range for twelve days. We dug our camp into the blue ice that formed the surface, and escaped most of it. But for twelve consecutive days the wind blew at forty-five miles an hour. It went as high as forty-eight, and fell to forty-one at times. The temperature was −63 degrees. It rose to −60 and fell to −68. It was meteorologically impossible, and it went on uninterruptedly for twelve days and twelve nights.

"Somewhere to the south, the frozen air of the South Polar Plateau slides down from that 18,000-foot bowl, down a mountain pass, over a glacier, and starts north. There must be a funneling mountain chain that directs it, and sweeps it away for four hundred miles to hit that bald plateau where we found the secondary pole, and 350 miles farther north reaches the Antarctic Ocean.

"It's been frozen there since Antarctica

froze twenty million years ago. There never
has been a thaw there.

"Twenty million years ago Antarctica was
beginning to freeze. We've investigated,
though, and built speculations. What we believe happened was about like this.

"Something came down out of space, a ship.
We saw it there in the blue ice, a thing like a
submarine without a conning tower or direc-
tive vanes, 280 feet long and 45 feet in di-
ameter at its thickest.

"Eh, Van Wall? Space? Yes, but I'll explain
that better later." McReady's steady voice
went on.

"It came down from space, driven and lifted
by forces men haven't discovered yet, and
somehow — perhaps something went wrong
then — it tangled with Earth's magnetic field.
It came south here, out of control probably,
circling the magnetic pole. That's a savage
country there, but when Antarctica was still
freezing, it must have been a thousand times
more savage. There must have been blizzard
snow, as well as drift, new snow falling as the
continent glaciated. The swirl there must have
been particularly bad, the wind hurling a solid
blanket of white over the lip of that now-
buried mountain.

"The ship struck solid granite head-on, and
cracked up. Not every one of the passengers
in it was killed, but the ship must have been
ruined, her driving mechanism locked. It
tangled with Earth's field, Norris believes. No
thing made by intelligent beings can tangle

with the dead immensity of a planet's natural forces and survive.

"One of its passengers stepped out. The wind we saw there never fell below forty-one, and the temperature never rose above —60. Then — the wind must have been stronger. And there was drift falling in a solid sheet. The *thing* was lost completely in ten paces." He paused for a moment, the deep, steady voice giving way to the drone of wind overhead and the uneasy, malicious gurgling in the pipe of the galley stove.

Drift — a drift-wind was sweeping by overhead. Right now the snow picked up by the mumbling wind fled in level, blinding lines across the face of the buried camp. If a man stepped out of the tunnels that connected each of the camp buildings beneath the surface, he'd be lost in ten paces. Out there, the slim, black finger of the radio mast lifted three hundred feet into the air, and at its peak was the clear night sky. A sky of thin, whining wind rushing steadily from beyond to another beyond under the licking, curling mantle of the aurora. And off north, the horizon flamed with queer, angry colors of the midnight twilight. That was Spring three hundred feet above Antarctica.

At the surface — it was white death. Death of a needle-fingered cold driven before the wind, sucking heat from any warm thing. Cold — and white mist of endless, everlasting drift, the fine, fine particles of licking snow that obscured all things.

Kinner, the little, scar-faced cook, winced. Five days ago he had stepped out to the surface to reach a cache of frozen beef. He had reached it, started back — and the drift-wind leapt out of the south. Cold, white death that streamed across the ground blinded him in twenty seconds. He stumbled on wildly in circles. It was half an hour before rope-guided men from below found him in the impenetrable murk.

It was easy for man — or *thing* — to get lost in ten paces.

"And the drift-wind then was probably more impenetrable than we know." McReady's voice snapped Kinner's mind back. Back to the welcome, dank warmth of the Ad Building. "The passenger of the ship wasn't prepared either, it appears. It froze within ten feet of the ship.

"We dug down to find the ship, and our tunnel happened to find the frozen — animal. Barclay's ice-ax struck its skull.

"When we saw what it was, Barclay went back to the tractor, started the fire up and when the steam pressure built, sent a call for Blair and Dr. Copper. Barclay himself was sick then. Stayed sick for three days, as a matter of fact.

"When Blair and Copper came, we cut out the animal in a block of ice, as you see, wrapped it and loaded it on the tractor for return here. We wanted to get into that ship.

"We reached the side and found the metal was something we didn't know. Our beryllium-bronze, non-magnetic tools wouldn't touch it.

Barclay had some tool-steel on the tractor, and that wouldn't scratch it either. We made reasonable tests — even tried some acid from the batteries with no results.

"They must have had a passivating process to make magnesium metal resist acid that way, and the alloy must have been at least ninety-five percent magnesium. But we had no way of guessing that, so when we spotted the barely opened lock door, we cut around it. There was clear, hard ice inside the lock, where we couldn't reach it. Through the little crack we could look in and see that only metal and tools were in there, so we decided to loosen the ice with a bomb.

"We had decanite bombs and thermite. Thermite is the ice-softener; decanite might have shattered valuable things, where the thermite's heat would just loosen the ice. Dr. Copper, Norris, and I placed a twenty-five-pound thermite bomb, wired it, and took the connector up the tunnel to the surface, where Blair had the steam tractor waiting. A hundred yards the other side of that granite wall we set off the thermite bomb.

"The magnesium metal of the ship caught of course. The glow of the bomb flared and died, then it began to flare again. We ran back to the tractor, and gradually the glare built up. From where we were we could see the whole ice-field illuminated from beneath with an unbearable light; the ship's shadow was a great, dark cone reaching off toward the north, where the twilight was just about gone.

For a moment it lasted, and we counted three other shadow-things that might have been other — passengers — frozen there. Then the ice was crashing down and against the ship.

"That's why I told you about that place. The wind sweeping down from the Pole was at our backs. Steam and hydrogen flame were torn away in white ice-fog; the flaming heat under the ice there was yanked away toward the Antarctic Ocean before it touched us. Otherwise we wouldn't have come back, even with the shelter of that granite ridge that stopped the light.

"Somehow in the blinding inferno we could see great hunched things — black hulks. They shed even the furious incandescence of the magnesium for a time. Those must have been the engines, we knew. Secrets going in blazing glory — secrets that might have given Man the planets. Mysterious things that could lift and hurl that ship — and had soaked in the force of the Earth's magnetic field. I saw Norris' mouth move, and ducked. I couldn't hear him.

"Insulation — something — gave way. All Earth's field they'd soaked up twenty million years before broke loose. The aurora in the sky above licked down, and the whole plateau there was bathed in cold fire that blanketed vision. The ice-ax in my hand got red hot, and hissed on the ice. Metal buttons on my clothes burned into me. And a flash of electric blue seared upward from beyond the granite wall.

"Then the walls of ice crashed down on it.

For an instant it squealed the way dry ice does when it's pressed between metal.

"We were blind and groping in the dark for hours while our eyes recovered. We found every coil within a mile was fused rubbish, the dynamo and every radio set, the earphones and speakers. If we hadn't had the steam tractor, we wouldn't have gotten over to the Secondary Camp.

"Van Wall flew in from Big Magnet at sunup, as you know. We came home as soon as possible. That is the history of — that." McReady's great bronze beard gestured toward the thing on the table.

2

Blair stirred uneasily, his little, bony fingers wriggling under the harsh light. Little brown freckles on his knuckles slid back and forth as the tendons under the skin twitched. He pulled aside a bit of the tarpaulin and looked impatiently at the dark ice-bound thing inside.

McReady's big body straightened somewhat. He'd ridden the rocking, jarring steam tractor forty miles that day, pushing on to Big Magnet here. Even his calm will had been pressed by the anxiety to mix again with humans. It was lone and quiet out there in Secondary Camp, where a wolf-wind howled down from the Pole. Wolf-wind howling in his sleep — winds droning and the evil, unspeakable face of that monster leering up as he'd first seen it through clear, blue ice, with a bronze ice-ax buried in its skull.

The giant meteorologist spoke again. "The problem is this. Blair wants to examine the thing. Thaw it out and make micro slides of its tissues and so forth. Norris doesn't believe that is safe, and Blair does. Dr. Copper agrees pretty much with Blair. Norris is a physicist, of course, not a biologist. But he makes a point I think we should all hear. Blair has described the microscopic life-forms biologists find living, even in this cold and inhospitable place. They freeze every winter, and thaw every summer — for three months — and live.

"The point Norris makes is — they thaw, and live again. There must have been microscopic life associated with this creature. There is with every living thing we know. And Norris is afraid that we may release a plague — some germ disease unknown to Earth — if we thaw those microscopic things that have been frozen there for twenty million years.

"Blair admits that such micro-life might retain the power of living. Such unorganized things as individual cells can retain life for unknown periods, when solidly frozen. The beast itself is as dead as those frozen mammoths they find in Siberia. Organized, highly developed life-forms can't stand that treatment.

"But micro-life could. Norris suggests that we may release some disease-form that man, never having met it before, will be utterly defenseless against.

"Blair's answer is that there may be such still-living germs, but that Norris has the case reversed. They are utterly nonimmune to man. Our life-chemistry probably — " ˙

"Probably!" The little biologist's head lifted in a quick, birdlike motion. The halo of gray hair about his bald head ruffled as though angry. "Heh, one look — "

"I know," McReady acknowledged. "The thing is not Earthly. It does not seem likely it can have a life-chemistry sufficiently like ours to make cross-infection remotely possible. I would say that there is no danger."

McReady looked toward Dr. Copper. The physician shook his head slowly. "None whatever," he asserted confidently. "Man cannot infect or be infected by germs that live in such comparatively close relatives as the snakes. And they are, I assure you," his clean-shaven face grimaced uneasily, "*much* nearer to us than — *that*."

Vance Norris moved angrily. He was comparatively short in this gathering of big men, some five feet eight, and his stocky, powerful build tended to make him seem shorter. His black hair was crisp and hard, like short, steel wires, and his eyes were the gray of fractured steel. If McReady was a man of bronze, Norris was all steel. His movements, his thoughts, his whole bearing had the quick, hard impulse of a steel spring. His nerves were steel — hard, quick acting — swift corroding.

He was decided on his point now, and he lashed out in its defense with a characteristic quick, clipped flow of words. "Different chemistry be damned. That thing may be dead — or, by God, it may not — but I don't like it. Damn it, Blair, let them see the monstrosity you are petting over there. Let them see the foul thing and decide for themselves whether they want that thing thawed out in this camp.

"Thawed out, by the way. That's got to be thawed out in one of the shacks tonight, if it is thawed out. Somebody — who's watchman tonight? Magnetic — oh, Connant. Cosmic rays tonight. Well, you get to sit up with that twenty-million-year-old mummy of his. Unwrap it, Blair. How the hell can they tell what they are buying, if they can't see it? It may have a different chemistry. I don't care what else it has, but I know it has something I don't want. If you can judge by the look on its face — it isn't human so maybe you can't — it was annoyed when it froze. Annoyed, in fact, is just about as close an approximation of the way it felt, as crazy, mad, insane hatred. Neither one touches the subject.

"How the hell can these birds tell what they are voting on? They haven't seen those three red eyes and that blue hair like crawling worms. Crawling — damn, it's crawling there in the ice right now!

"Nothing Earth ever spawned had the unutterable sublimation of devastating wrath that thing let loose in its face when it looked around its frozen desolation twenty million

years ago. Mad? It was mad clear through —
searing, blistering mad!

"Hell, I've had bad dreams ever since I
looked at those three red eyes. Nightmares.
Dreaming the thing thawed out and came to
life — that it wasn't dead, or even wholly unconscious all those twenty million years, but
just slowed, waiting — waiting. You'll dream,
too, while that damned thing that Earth
wouldn't own is dripping, dripping in the
Cosmos House tonight.

"And, Connant," Norris whipped toward the
cosmic ray specialist, "won't you have fun
sitting up all night in the quiet. Wind whining
above — and that thing dripping — " he
stopped for a moment, and looked around.

"I know. That's not science. But this is, it's
psychology. You'll have nightmares for a year
to come. Every night since I looked at that
thing I've had 'em. That's why I hate it — sure
I do — and don't want it around. Put it back
where it came from and let it freeze for another twenty million years. I had some swell
nightmares — that it wasn't made like we are
— which is obvious — but of a different kind
of flesh that it can really control. That it can
change its shape, and look like a man — and
wait to kill and eat —

"That's not a logical argument. I know it
isn't. The thing isn't Earth-logic anyway.

"Maybe it has an alien body-chemistry, and
maybe its bugs do have a different body-
chemistry. A germ might not stand that, but,
Blair and Copper, how about a virus? That's

just an enzyme molecule, you've said. That wouldn't need anything but a protein molecule of any body to work on.

"And how are you so sure that, of the million varieties of microscopic life it may have, *none* of them are dangerous? How about diseases like hydrophobia — rabies — that attack any warm-blooded creature, whatever its body-chemistry may be? And parrot fever? Have you a body like a parrot, Blair? And plain rot — gangrene — necrosis if you want? *That* isn't choosy about body chemistry!"

Blair looked up from his puttering long enough to meet Norris' angry, gray eyes for an instant. "So far the only thing you have said this thing gave off that was catching was dreams. I'll go so far as to admit that." An impish, slightly malignant grin crossed the little man's seamed face. "I had some, too. So. It's dream-infectious. No doubt an exceedingly dangerous malady.

"So far as your other things go, you have a badly mistaken idea about viruses. In the first place, nobody has shown that the enzyme-molecule theory, and that alone, explains them. And in the second place, when you catch tobacco mosaic or wheat rust, let me know. A wheat plant is a lot nearer your body-chemistry than this other-world creature is.

"And your rabies is limited, strictly limited. You can't get it from, nor give it to, a wheat plant or a fish — which is a collateral descendant of a common ancestor of yours. Which this, Norris, is not." Blair nodded pleasantly toward the tarpaulined bulk on the table.

"Well, thaw the damned thing in a tub of formalin if you must. I've suggested that—"

"And I've said there would be no sense in it. You can't compromise. Why did you and Commander Garry come down here to study magnetism? Why weren't you content to stay at home? There's magnetic force enough in New York. I could no more study the life this thing once had from a formalin-pickled sample than you could get the information you wanted back in New York. And—if this one is so treated, *never in all time to come can there be a duplicate!* The race it came from must have passed away in the twenty million years it lay frozen, so that even if it came from Mars, then, we'd never find its like. And— the ship is gone.

"There's only one way to do this—and that is the best possible way. It must be thawed slowly, carefully, and not in formalin."

Commander Garry stood forward again, and Norris stepped back muttering angrily. "I think Blair is right, gentlemen. What do you say?"

Connant grunted. "It sounds right to us, I think—only perhaps he ought to stand watch over it while it's thawing." He grinned ruefully, brushing a stray lock of ripe-cherry hair back from his forehead. "Swell idea, in fact— if he sits up with his jolly little corpse."

Garry smiled slightly. A general chuckle of

agreement rippled over the group. "I should think any ghost it may have had would have starved to death if it hung around here that long, Connant," Garry suggested. "And you look capable of taking care of it. 'Ironman' Connant ought to be able to take out any opposing players, still."

Connant shook himself uneasily. "I'm not worrying about ghosts. Let's see that thing. I —"

Eagerly Blair was stripping back the ropes. A single throw of the tarpaulin revealed the thing. The ice had melted somewhat in the heat of the room, and it was clear and blue as thick, good glass. It shone wet and sleek under the harsh light of the unshielded globe above.

The room stiffened abruptly. It was face up there on the plain, greasy planks of the table. The broken haft of the bronze ice-axe was still buried in the queer skull. Three mad, hate-filled eyes blazed up with a living fire, bright as fresh-spilled blood, from a face ringed with a writhing, loathsome nest of worms, blue, mobile worms that crawled where hair should grow —

Van Wall, six feet and two hundred pounds of ice-nerved pilot, gave a queer, strangled gasp, and butted, stumbled his way out to the corridor. Half the company broke for the doors. The others stumbled away from the table.

McReady stood at the end of the table watching them, his great body planted solid

on his powerful legs. Norris from the opposite
end glowered at the thing with smouldering
hate. Outside the door, Garry was talking with
half a dozen of the men at once.

Blair had a tack hammer. The ice that cased
the thing *schluffed* crisply under its steel
claw as it peeled from the thing it had cased
for twenty million years —

3

"I know you don't like the thing, Connant,
but it just has to be thawed out right. You say
leave it as it is till we get back to civilization.
All right, I'll admit your argument that we
could do a better and more complete job there
is sound. But — how are we going to get this
across the Line? We have to take this through
one temperate zone, the equatorial zone, and
halfway through the other temperate zone before we get it to New York. You don't want to
sit with it one night, but you suggest, then,
that I hang its corpse in the freezer with the
beef?" Blair looked up from his cautious chipping, his bald freckled skull nodding trium-
phantly.

Kinner, the stocky, scar-faced cook, saved
Connant the trouble of answering. "Hey, you
listen, mister. You put that thing in the box
with the meat, and by all the gods there ever
were, I'll put you in to keep it company. You
birds have brought everything movable in this

camp in onto my mess tables here already, and I had to stand for that. But you go putting things like that in my meat box, or even my meat cache here, and you cook your own damn grub."

"But, Kinner, this is the only table in Big Magnet that's big enough to work on," Blair objected. "Everybody's explained that."

"Yeah, and everybody's brought everything in here. Clark brings his dogs every time there's a fight and sews them up on that table. Ralsen brings in his sledges. Hell, the only thing you haven't had on that table is the Boeing. And you'd 'a' had that in if you coulda figured a way to get it through the tunnels."

Commander Garry chuckled and grinned at Van Wall, the huge Chief Pilot. Van Wall's great blond beard twitched suspiciously as he nodded gravely to Kinner. "You're right, Kinner. The aviation department is the only one that treats you right."

"It does get crowded, Kinner," Garry acknowledged. "But I'm afraid we all find it that way at times. Not much privacy in an Antarctic camp."

"Privacy? What the hell's that? You know, the thing that really made me weep was when I saw Barclay marchin' through here chantin' 'The last lumber in the camp! The last lumber in the camp!' and carryin' it out to build that house on his tractor. Damn it, I missed that moon cut in the door he carried out more'n I missed the sun when it set. That wasn't just the last lumber Barclay was walkin' off with. He was carryin' off the last bit of privacy in this blasted place."

A grin rode even on Connant's heavy face as Kinner's perennial, good-natured grouch came up again. But it died away quickly as his dark, deepset eyes turned again to the red-eyed thing Blair was chipping from its cocoon of ice. A big hand ruffed his shoulder-length hair, and tugged at a twisted lock that fell behind his ear in a familiar gesture. "I know that cosmic ray shack's going to be too crowded if I have to sit up with that thing," he growled. "Why can't you go on chipping the ice away from around it — you can do that without anybody butting in, I assure you — and then hang the thing up over the power-plant boiler? That's warm enough. It'll thaw out a chicken, even a whole side of beef, in a few hours."

"I know," Blair protested, dropping the tack hammer to gesture more effectively with his bony, freckled fingers, his small body tense with eagerness, "but this is too important to take any chances. There never was a find like this; there never can be again. It's the only chance men will ever have, and it has to be done exactly right.

"Look, you know how the fish we caught down near the Ross Sea would freeze almost as soon as we got them on deck, and come to life again if we thawed them gently? Low forms of life aren't killed by quick freezing and slow thawing. We have — "

"Hey, for the love of Heaven — you mean

that damned thing will come to life!" Connant yelled. "You get the damned thing — Let me at it! That's going to be in so many pieces — "

"No! *No*, you fool — " Blair jumped in front of Connant to protect his precious find. "No. Just *low* forms of life. For Pete's sake let me finish. You can't thaw higher forms of life and have them come to. Wait a moment now — hold it! A fish can come to after freezing because it's so low a form of life that the individual cells of its body can revive, and that alone is enough to reestablish life. Any higher forms thawed out that way are dead. Though the individual cells revive, they die because there must be organization and cooperative effort to live. That cooperation cannot be reestablished. There is a sort of potential life in any uninjured, quick-frozen animal. But it can't — can't under any circumstances — become active life in higher animals. The higher animals are too complex, too delicate. This is an intelligent creature as high in its evolution as we are in ours. Perhaps higher. It is as dead as a frozen man would be."

"How do you know?" demanded Connant, hefting the ice-ax he had seized a moment before.

Commander Garry laid a restraining hand on his heavy shoulder. "Wait a minute, Connant. I want to get this straight. I agree that there is going to be no thawing of this thing if there is the remotest chance of its revival. I quite agree it is much too unpleasant to have alive, but I had no idea there was the remotest possibility."

Dr. Copper pulled his pipe from between his teeth and heaved his stocky, dark body from the bunk he had been sitting in. "Blair's being technical. That's dead. As dead as the mammoths they find frozen in Siberia. We have all sorts of proof that things don't live after being frozen — not even fish, generally speaking — and no proof that higher animal life can under any circumstances. What's the point, Blair?"

The little biologist shook himself. The little ruff of hair standing out around his bald pate waved in righteous anger. "The point is," he said in an injured tone, "that the individual cells might show the characteristics they had in life if it is properly thawed. A man's muscle cells live many hours after he has died. Just because they live, and a few things like hair and fingernail cells still live, you wouldn't accuse a corpse of being a zombie, or something.

"Now if I thaw this right, I may have a chance to determine what sort of world it's native to. We don't, and can't know by any other means, whether it came from Earth or Mars or Venus or from beyond the stars.

"And just because it looks unlike men, you don't have to accuse it of being evil, or vicious, or something. Maybe that expression on its face is its equivalent to a resignation to fate. White is the color of mourning to the

Chinese. If men can have different customs, why can't a so-different race have different understandings of facial expressions?"

Connant laughed softly, mirthlessly. "Peaceful resignation! If that is the best it could do in the way of resignation, I should exceedingly dislike seeing it when it was looking mad. That face was never designed to express peace. It just didn't have any philosophical thoughts like peace in its make-up.

"I know it's your pet — but be sane about it. That thing grew up on evil, adolesced slowly roasting alive the local equivalent of kittens, and amused itself through maturity on new and ingenious torture."

"You haven't the slightest right to say that," snapped Blair. "How do you know the first thing about the meaning of a facial expression inherently inhuman? It may well have no human equivalent whatever. That is just a different development of Nature, another example of Nature's wonderful adaptability. Growing on another, perhaps harsher world, it has different form and features. But it is just as much a legitimate child of Nature as you are. You are displaying that childish human weakness of hating the different. On its own world it would probably class you as a fish-belly, white monstrosity with an insufficient number of eyes and a fungoid body pale and bloated with gas.

"Just because its nature is different, you haven't any right to say it's necessarily evil."

Norris burst out a single, explosive, "Haw!" He looked down at the thing. "May be that things from other worlds don't *have* to be evil just because they're different. But that thing *was!* Child of Nature, eh? Well, it was a hell of an evil Nature."

"Aw, will you mugs cut crabbing at each other and get the damned thing off my table?" Kinner growled. "And put a canvas over it. It looks indecent."

"Kinner's gone modest," jeered Connant.

Kinner slanted his eyes up to the big physicist. The scarred cheek twisted to join the line of his tight lips in a twisted grin. "All right, big boy, and what were you grousing about a minute ago? We can set the thing in a chair next to you tonight, if you want."

"I'm not afraid of its face," Connant snapped. "I don't like keeping a wake over its corpse particularly, but I'm going to do it."

Kinner's grin spread. "Uh-huh." He went off to the galley stove and shook down ashes vigorously, drowning the brittle chipping of the ice as Blair fell to work again.

4

"*Cluck,*" reported the cosmic-ray counter, "*cluck-burrrp-cluck.*"

Connant started and dropped his pencil.

"Damnation." The physicist looked toward the far corner, back at the Geiger counter on the table near that corner. And crawled under

the desk at which he had been working to
retrieve the pencil. He sat down at his work
again, trying to make his writing more even.
It tended to have jerks and quavers in it, in
time with the abrupt proud-hen noises of the
Geiger counter. The muted whoosh of the
pressure lamp he was using for illumination,
the mingled gargles and bugle calls of a dozen
men sleeping down the corridor in Paradise
House formed the background sounds for the
irregular, clucking noises of the counter, the
occasional rustle of falling coal in the copper-
bellied stove. And a soft, steady *drip-drip-drip*
from the thing in the corner.

Connant jerked a pack of cigarettes from
his pocket, snapped it so that a cigarette
protruded, and jabbed the cylinder into his
mouth. The lighter failed to function, and he
pawed angrily through the pile of papers in
search of a match. He scratched the wheel of
the lighter several times, dropped it with a
curse and got up to pluck a hot coal from the
stove with the coal tongs.

The lighter functioned instantly when he
tried it on returning to the desk. The counter
ripped out a series of chuckling guffaws as a
burst of cosmic rays struck through to it.
Connant turned to glower at it, and tried to
concentrate on the interpretation of data collected during the past week. The weekly sum-
mary —

He gave up and yielded to curiosity, or
nervousness. He lifted the pressure lamp from
the desk and carried it over to the table in the

corner. Then he returned to the stove and picked up the coal tongs. The beast had been thawing for nearly eighteen hours now. He poked at it with an unconscious caution; the flesh was no longer hard as armor plate, but had assumed a rubbery texture. It looked like wet, blue rubber glistening under droplets of water like little round jewels in the glare of the gasoline pressure lantern. Connant felt an unreasoning desire to pour the contents of the lamp's reservoir over the thing in its box and drop the cigarette into it. The three red eyes glared up at him sightlessly, the ruby eyeballs reflecting murky, smoky rays of light.

He realized vaguely that he had been looking at them for a very long time, even vaguely understood that they were no longer sightless. But it did not seem of importance, of no more importance than the labored, slow motion of the tentacular things that sprouted from the base of the scrawny, slowly pulsing neck.

Connant picked up the pressure lamp and returned to his chair. He sat down, staring at the pages of mathematics before him. The clucking of the counter was strangely less disturbing, the rustle of the coals in the stove no longer distracting.

The creak of the floorboards behind him didn't interrupt his thoughts as he went about his weekly report in an automatic manner, filling in columns of data and making brief, summarizing notes.

The creak of the floorboards sounded nearer.

5

Blair came up from the nightmare-haunted depths of sleep abruptly. Connant's face floated vaguely above him; for a moment it seemed a continuance of the wild horror of the dream. But Connant's face was angry, and a little frightened. "Blair — Blair you damned log, wake up."

"Uh-eh?" the little biologist rubbed his eyes, his bony, freckled finger crooked to a mutilated child-fist. From surrounding bunks other faces lifted to stare down at them.

Connant straightened up. "Get up — and get a lift on. Your damned animal's escaped."

"Escaped — what!" Chief Pilot Van Wall's bull voice roared out with a volume that shook the walls. Down the communication tunnels other voices yelled suddenly. The dozen inhabitants of Paradise House tumbled in abruptly, Barclay, stocky and bulbous in long woolen underwear, carrying a fire extinguisher.

"What the hell's the matter?" Barclay demanded.

"Your damned beast got loose. I fell asleep about twenty minutes ago, and when I woke up, the thing was gone. Hey, Doc, the hell you say those things can't come to life. Blair's blasted potential life developed a hell of a lot of potential and walked out on us."

Copper stared blankly. "It wasn't — Earthly," he sighed suddenly. "I — I guess Earthly laws don't apply."

"Well, it applied for leave of absence and took it. We've got to find it and capture it somehow." Connant swore bitterly, his deep-set black eyes sullen and angry. "It's a wonder the hellish creature didn't eat me in my sleep."

Blair started back, his pale eyes suddenly fear-struck. "Maybe it di — er — uh — we'll have to find it."

"You find it. It's your pet. I've had all I want to do with it, sitting there for seven hours with the counter clucking every few seconds, and you birds in here singing night-music. It's a wonder I got to sleep. I'm going through to the Ad Building."

Commander Garry ducked through the doorway, pulling his belt tight. "You won't have to. Van's roar sounded like the Boeing taking off downwind. So it wasn't dead?"

"I didn't carry it off in my arms, I assure you," Connant snapped. "The last I saw, the split skull was oozing green goo, like a squashed caterpillar. Doc just said our laws don't work — it's unearthly. Well, it's an un-earthly monster, with an unearthly disposition, judging by the face, wandering around with a split skull and brains oozing out." Norris and McReady appeared in the doorway, a doorway filling with other shivering men. "Has anybody seen it coming over here?" Norris asked in-nocently. "About four feet tall — three red eyes — brains oozing out — Hey, has any-body checked to make sure this isn't a cracked idea of humor? It it is, I think we'll unite in tying Blair's pet around Connant's neck like the Ancient Mariner's albatross."

"It's no humor," Connant shivered. "Lord, I wish it were. I'd rather wear — " He stopped. A wild, weird howl shrieked through the corridors. The men stiffened abruptly, and half turned.

"I think it's been located," Connant finished. His dark eyes shifted with a queer unease. He darted back to his bunk in Paradise House, to return almost immediately with a heavy .45 revolver and an ice-ax. He hefted both gently as he started for the corridor toward Dogtown.

"It blundered down the wrong corridor — and landed among the huskies. Listen — the dogs have broken their chains — "

The half-terrorized howl of the dog pack had changed to a wild hunting melee. The voices of the dogs thundered in the narrow corridors, and through them came a low rippling snarl of distilled hate. A shrill of pain, a dozen snarling yelps.

Connant broke for the door. Close behind him, McReady, then Barclay and Commander Garry came. Other men broke for the Ad Building, and weapons — the sledge house. Pomroy, in charge of Big Magnet's five cows, started down the corridor in the opposite direction — he had a six-foot-handled, long-tined pitchfork in mind.

Barclay slid to a halt, as McReady's giant bulk turned abruptly away from the tunnel leading to Dogtown, and vanished off at an angle. Uncertainly, the mechanician wavered

a moment, the fire extinguisher in his hands,
hesitating from one side to the other. Then he
was racing after Connant's broad back. Whatever McReady had in mind, he could be trusted
to make it work.

Connant stopped at the bend in the corridor.
His breath hissed suddenly through his throat.
"Great God — " The revolver exploded thun-
derously; three numbing, palpable waves of
sound crashed through the confined corridors.
Two more. The revolver dropped to the hard-
packed snow of the trail, and Barclay saw the
ice-ax shift into defensive position. Connant's
powerful body blocked his vision, but beyond
he heard something mewing, and, insanely,
chuckling. The dogs were quieter; there was a
deadly seriousness in their low snarls. Taloned
feet scratched at hard-packed snow, broken
chains were clinking and tangling.

Connant shifted abruptly, and Barclay could
see what lay beyond. For a second he stood
frozen, then his breath went out in a gusty
curse. The Thing launched itself at Connant,
the powerful arms of the man swung the ice-ax
flat-side first at what might have been a head.
It scrunched horribly, and the tattered flesh,
ripped by a half-dozen savage huskies, leapt
to its feet again. The red eyes blazed with an
unearthly hatred, an unearthly unkillable
vitality.

Barclay turned the fire extinguisher on it;
the blinding, blistering stream of chemical
spray confused it, baffled it, together with the
savage attacks of the huskies, not for long

afraid of anything that did, or could live, and
held it at bay.

McReady wedged men out of his way and
drove down the narrow corridor packed with
men unable to reach the scene. There was a
foreplanned drive to McReady's attack. One
of the giant blowtorches used in warming the
plane's engines was in his bronzed hands. It
roared gustily as he turned the corner and
opened the valve. The mad mewing hissed
louder. The dogs scrambled back from the
three-foot lance of blue-hot flame.

"Bar, get a power cable, run it in somehow.
And a handle. We can electrocute this —
monster, if I don't incinerate it." McReady
spoke with an authority of planned action.
Barclay turned down the long corridor to the
power plant, but already before him Norris
and Van Wall were racing down.

Barclay found the cable in the electrical
cache in the tunnel wall. In a half minute he
was hacking at it, walking back. Van Wall's
voice rang out in warning shout of "Power!"
as the emergency gasoline-powered dynamo
thudded into action. Half a dozen other men
were down there now; the coal, kindling were
going into the firebox of the steam power
plant. Norris, cursing in a low, deadly monotone, was working with quick, sure fingers on
the other end of Barclay's cable, splicing a
contactor into one of the power leads.

The dogs had fallen back when Barclay
reached the corridor bend, fallen back before
a furious monstrosity that glared from baleful

red eyes, mewing in trapped hatred. The dogs were a semicircle of red-dipped muzzles with a fringe of glistening white teeth, whining with a vicious eagerness that near matched the fury of the red eyes. McReady stood confidently alert at the corridor bend, the gustily muttering torch held loose and ready for action in his hands. He stepped aside without moving his eyes from the beast as Barclay came up. There was a slight, tight smile on his lean, bronzed face.

Norris' voice called down the corridor, and Barclay stepped forward. The cable was taped to the long handle of a snow shovel, the two conductors split and held eighteen inches apart by a scrap of lumber lashed at right angles across the far end of the handle. Bare copper conductors, charged with 220 volts, glinted in the light of pressure lamps. The Thing mewed and hated and dodged. McReady advanced to Barclay's side. The dogs beyond sensed the plan with the almost telepathic intelligence of trained huskies. Their whining grew shriller, softer, their mincing steps carried them nearer. Abruptly a huge night-black Alaskan leapt into the trapped thing. It turned squalling, saber-clawed feet slashing.

Barclay leapt forward and jabbed. A weird, shrill scream rose and choked out. The smell of burnt flesh in the corridor intensified; greasy smoke curled up. The echoing pound of the gas-electric dynamo down the corridor became a slogging thud.

The red eyes clouded over in a stiffening,

jerking travesty of a face. Armlike, leglike members quivered and jerked. The dogs leapt forward, and Barclay yanked back his shovel-handle weapon. The thing on the snow did not move as gleaming teeth ripped it open.

6

Garry looked about the crowded room. Thirty-two men, some tensed nervously standing against the wall, some uneasily relaxed, some sitting, most perforce standing as intimate as sardines. Thirty-two, plus the five engaged in sewing up wounded dogs, made thirty-seven, the total personnel.

Garry started speaking. "All right, I guess we're here. Some of you — three or four at most — saw what happened. All of you have seen that thing on the table, and can get a general idea. Anyone hasn't, I'll lift — " His hand strayed to the tarpaulin bulking over the thing on the table. There was an acrid odor of singed flesh seeping out of it. The men stirred restlessly, hasty denials.

"It looks rather as though Charnauk isn't going to lead any more teams," Garry went on. "Blair wants to get at this thing, and make some more detailed examination. We want to know what happened, and make sure right now that this is permanently, totally dead. Right?"

Connant grinned. "Anybody that doesn't can sit up with it tonight."

"All right then, Blair, what can you say about it? What was it?" Garry turned to the little biologist.

"I wonder if we ever saw its natural form," Blair looked at the covered mass. "It may have been imitating the beings that built that ship — but I don't think it was. I think that was its true form. Those of us who were up near the bend saw the thing in action; the thing on the table is the result. When it got loose, apparently, it started looking around. Antarctica still frozen as it was ages ago when the creature first saw it — and froze. From my observations while it was thawing out, and the bits of tissue I cut and hardened then, I think it was native to a hotter planet than Earth. It couldn't, in its natural form, stand the temperature. There is no life-form on Earth that can live in Antarctica during the winter, but the best compromise is the dog. It found the dogs, and somehow got near enough to Charnauk to get him. The others smelled it — heard it — I don't know — anyway they went wild, and broke chains, and attacked it before it was finished. The thing we found was part Charnauk, queerly only half-dead, part Charnauk half-digested by the jellylike protoplasm of that creature, and part the remains of the thing we originally found, sort of melted down to the basic protoplasm.

"When the dogs attacked it, it turned into the best fighting thing it could think of. Some other-world beast apparently."

"Turned," snapped Garry. "How?"

"Every living thing is made up of jelly —
protoplasm and minute, submicroscopic things
called nuclei, which control the bulk, the protoplasm. This thing was just a modification of
that same world-wide plan of Nature; cells
made up of protoplasm, controlled by infinitely tinier nuclei. You physicists might
compare it — an individual cell of any living
thing — with an atom; the bulk of the atom,
the space-filling part, is made up of the elec-
tron orbits, but the character of the thing is
determined by the atomic nucleus.

"This isn't wildly beyond what we already
know. It's just a modification we haven't seen
before. It's as natural, as logical, as any other
manifestation of life. It obeys exactly the
same laws. The cells are made of protoplasm,
their character determined by the nucleus.

"Only, in this creature, the cell nuclei can
control those cells *at will.* It digested Charnauk, and as it digested, studied every cell of
his tissue, and shaped its own cells to imitate
them exactly. Parts of it — parts that had
time to finish changing — are dog-cells. But
they don't have dog-cell nuclei." Blair lifted a
fraction of the tarpaulin. A torn dog's leg,
with stiff gray fur protruded. "That, for instance, isn't a dog at all, it's imitation. Some
parts I'm uncertain about; the nucleus was
hiding itself, covering up with dog-cell imitation nucleus. In time, not even a microscope
would have shown the difference."

"Suppose," asked Norris bitterly, "it had
had lots of time?"

"Then it would have been a dog. The other dogs would have accepted it. We would have accepted it. I don't think anything would have distinguished it, not microscope, nor X-ray, nor any other means. This is a member of a supremely intelligent race, a race that has learned the deepest secrets of biology, and turned them to its use."

"What was it planning to do?" Barclay looked at the humped tarpaulin.

Blair grinned unpleasantly. The wavering halo of thin hair round his bald pate wavered in a stir of air. "Take over the world, I imagine."

"Take over the world! Just it, all by itself?" Connant gasped. "Set itself up as a lone dictator?"

"No," Blair shook his head. The scalpel he had been fumbling in his bony fingers dropped; he bent to pick it up, so that his face was hidden as he spoke. "It would become the population of the world."

"Become — populate the world? Does it reproduce asexually?"

Blair shook his head and gulped. "It's — it doesn't have to. It weighed eighty-five pounds. Charnauk weighed about ninety. It would have become Charnauk, and had eighty-five pounds left, to become — oh, Jack for instance, or Chinook. It can imitate anything — that is, become anything. If it had reached the Antarctic Sea, it would have become a seal, maybe two seals. They might have attacked a killer whale, and become either killers, or a herd of seals.

Or maybe it would have caught an albatross, or a skua gull, and flown to South America."

Norris cursed softly. "And every time it digested something, and imitated it — "

"It would have had its original bulk left, to start again," Blair finished. "Nothing would kill it. It has no natural enemies, because it becomes whatever it wants to. If a killer whale attacked it, it would become a killer whale. If it was an albatross, and an eagle attacked it, it would become an eagle. Lord, it might become a female eagle. Go back — build a nest and lay eggs!"

"Are you sure that thing from hell is dead?" Dr. Copper asked softly.

"Yes, thank Heaven," the little biologist gasped. "After they drove the dogs off, I stood there poking Bar's electrocution thing into it for five minutes. It's dead and — cooked."

"Then we can only give thanks that this is Antarctica, where there is not one, single, solitary, living thing for it to imitate, except these animals in camp."

"Us," Blair giggled. "It can imitate us. Dogs can't make four hundred miles to the sea; there's no food. There aren't any skua gulls to imitate at this season. There aren't any penguins this far inland. There's nothing that can reach the sea from this point — except us. We've got brains. We can do it. Don't you see — *it's got to imitate us* — *it's got to be one of us* — *that's the only way it can fly an airplane*

— fly a plane for two hours, and rule — be — all Earth's inhabitants. A world for the taking *— if it imitates us!*

"It didn't know yet. It hadn't had a chance to learn. It was rushed — hurried — took the thing nearest its own size. Look — I'm Pandora! I opened the box! And the only hope that can come out is — that nothing can come out. You didn't see me. I did it. I fixed it. I smashed every magneto. Not a plane can fly. Nothing can fly." Blair giggled and lay down on the floor crying.

Chief Pilot Van Wall made for the door. His feet were fading echoes in the corridors as Dr. Copper bent unhurriedly over the little man on the floor. From his office at the end of the room he brought something and injected a solution into Blair's arm. "He might come out of it when he wakes up," he sighed, rising. McReady helped him lift the biologist onto a nearby bunk. "It all depends on whether we can convince him that thing is dead."

Van Wall ducked into the shack, brushing his heavy blond beard absently. "I didn't think a biologist would do a thing like that up thoroughly. He missed the spares in the second cache. It's all right. I smashed them."

Commander Garry nodded. "I was wondering about the radio."

Dr. Copper snorted. "You don't think it can leak out on a radio wave do you? You'd have five rescue attempts in the next three months if you stop the broadcasts. The thing to do is talk loud and not make a sound. Now I wonder — "

McReady looked speculatively at the doctor. "It might be like an infectious disease. Everything that drank any of its blood — "

Copper shook his head. "Blair missed something. Imitate it may, but it has, to a certain extent, its own body chemistry, its own metabolism. If it didn't, it would become a dog — and be a dog and nothing more. It has to be an imitation dog. Therefore you can detect it by serum tests. And its chemistry, since it comes from another world, must be so wholly, radically different that a few cells, such as gained by drops of blood, would be treated as disease germs by the dog, or human body."

"Blood — would one of those imitations bleed?" Norris demanded.

"Surely. Nothing mystic about blood. Muscle is about 90 percent water; blood differs only in having a couple percent more water, and less connective tissue. They'd bleed all right," Copper assured him.

Blair sat up in his bunk suddenly. "Connant — where's Connant?"

The physicist moved over toward the little biologist. "Here I am. What do you want?"

"Are you?" giggled Blair. He lapsed back into the bunk contorted with silent laughter.

Connant looked at him blankly. "Huh? Am I what?"

"*Are* you there?" Blair burst into gales of laughter. "*Are* you Connant? The beast wanted to be *man* — not a dog — "

7

Dr. Copper rose wearily from the bunk, and washed the hypodermic carefully. The little tinkles it made seemed loud in the packed room, now that Blair's gurgling laughter had finally quieted. Copper looked toward Garry and shook his head slowly. "Hopeless, I'm afraid. I don't think we can ever convince him the thing is dead now."

Norris laughed uncertainly. "I'm not sure you can convince me. Oh, damn you, McReady."

"McReady?" Commander Garry turned to look from Norris to McReady curiously.

"The nightmares," Norris explained. "He had a theory about the nightmares we had at the Secondary Station after finding that thing."

"And that was?" Garry looked at McReady levelly.

Norris answered for him, jerkily, uneasily. "That the creature wasn't dead, had a sort of enormously slowed existence, an existence that permitted it, nonetheless, to be vaguely aware of the passing of time, of our coming, after endless years. I had a dream it could imitate things."

"Well," Copper grunted, "it can."

"Don't be an ass," Norris snapped. "That's not what's bothering me. In the dream it could read minds, read thoughts and ideas and mannerisms."

"What's so bad about that? It seems to be worrying you more than the thought of the joy we're going to have with a madman in an Antarctic camp." Copper nodded toward Blair's sleeping form.

McReady shook his great head slowly. "You know that Connant is Connant, because he not merely looks like Connant — which we're beginning to believe that beast might be able to do — but he thinks like Connant, moves himself around as Connant does. That takes more than merely a body that looks like him; that takes Connant's own mind, and thoughts and mannerisms. Therefore, though you know that the thing might make itself *look* like Connant, you aren't much bothered, because you know it has a mind from another world, a totally unhuman mind, that couldn't possibly react and think and talk like a man we know, and do it so well as to fool us for a moment. The idea of the creature imitating one of us is fascinating, but unreal, because it is too completely unhuman to deceive us. It doesn't have a human mind."

"As I said before," Norris repeated, looking steadily at McReady, "you can say the damnedest things at the damnedest times. Will you be so good as to finish that thought — one way or the other?"

Kinner, the scar-faced expedition cook, had been standing near Connant. Suddenly he moved down the length of the crowded room toward his familiar galley. He shook the ashes from the galley stove noisily.

"It would do it no good," said Dr. Copper, softly as though thinking out loud, "to merely look like something it was trying to imitate; it would have to understand its feelings, its reactions. It *is* unhuman; it has powers of imitation beyond any conception of man. A good actor, by training himself, can imitate another man, another man's mannerisms, well enough to fool most people. Of course no actor could imitate so perfectly as to deceive men who had been living with the imitated one in the complete lack of privacy of an Antarctic camp. That would take a superhuman skill."

"Oh, you've got the bug, too?" Norris cursed softly.

Connant, standing alone at one end of the room, looked about him wildly, his face white. A gentle eddying of the men had crowded them slowly down toward the other end of the room, so that he stood quite alone. "My God, will you two Jeremiahs shut up?" Connant's voice shook. "What am I? Some kind of a microscopic specimen you're dissecting? Some unpleasant worm you're discussing in the third person?"

McReady looked up at him; his slowly twisting hands stopped for a moment. "Having a lovely time. Wish you were here. Signed: Everybody.

"Connant, if you think you're having a hell of a time, just move over on the other end for a while. You've got one thing we haven't; you know what the answer is. I'll tell you this, right now you're the most feared and respected man in Big Magnet."

"Lord, I wish you could see your eyes,"

Connant gasped. "Stop staring, will you! What the hell are you going to do?"

"Have you any suggestions, Dr. Copper?" Commander Garry asked steadily. "The present situation is impossible."

"Oh, is it?" Connant snapped. "Come over here and look at that crowd. By Heaven, they look exactly like that gang of huskies around the corridor bend. Benning, will you stop hefting that damned ice-ax?"

The coppery blade rang on the floor as the aviation mechanic nervously dropped it. He bent over and picked it up instantly, hefting it slowly, turning it in his hands, his brown eyes moving jerkily about the room.

Copper sat down on the bunk beside Blair. The wood creaked noisily in the room. Far down a corridor, a dog yelped in pain, and the dog drivers' tense voices floated softly back. "Microscopic examination," said the doctor thoughtfully, "would be useless, as Blair pointed out. Considerable time has passed. However, serum tests would be definitive."

"Serum tests? What do you mean exactly?" Commander Garry asked.

"If I had a rabbit that had been injected with human blood — a poison to rabbits, of course, as is the blood of any animal save that of another rabbit — and the injections continued in increasing doses for some time, the rabbit would be human-immune. If a small quantity of its blood were drawn off, allowed to separate in a test tube, and to the clear serum, a bit of human blood were added, there would be a visible reaction, proving the blood was human. If cow, or dog blood were added — or any protein material other than that one thing, human blood — no reaction would take place. That would prove definitely."

"Can you suggest where I might catch a rabbit for you, Doc?" Norris asked. "That is, nearer than Australia; we don't want to waste time going that far."

"I know there aren't any rabbits in Antarctica," Copper nodded, "but that is simply the usual animal. Any animal except man will do. A dog for instance. But it will take several days, and due to the greater size of the animal, considerable blood. Two of us will have to contribute."

"Would I do?" Garry asked.

"That will make two," Copper nodded. "I'll get to work on it right away."

"What about Connant in the meantime," Kinner demanded. "I'm going out that door and head off for the Ross Sea before I cook for him."

"He may be human — " Copper started.

Connant burst out in a flood of curses. "Human! *May* be human, you damned saw bones! What in hell do you think I am?"

"A monster," Copper snapped sharply. "Now shut up and listen." Connant's face drained of color and he sat down heavily as the indictment was put in words. "Until we know — you know as well as we do that we have reason to question the fact, and only you know how that question is to be answered —

we may reasonably be expected to lock you up. If you are — unhuman — you're a lot more dangerous than poor Blair there, and I'm going to see that he's locked up thoroughly. I expect that his next stage will be a violent desire to kill you, all the dogs, and probably all of us. When he wakes, he will be convinced we're all unhuman, and nothing on the planet will ever change his conviction. It would be kinder to let him die, but we can't do that, of course. He's going in one shack, and you can stay in Cosmos House with your cosmic ray apparatus. Which is about what you'd do anyway. I've got to fix up a couple of dogs."

Connant nodded bitterly. "I'm human. Hurry that test. Your eyes — Lord, I wish you could see your eyes staring — "

Commander Garry watched anxiously as Clark, the dog-handler, held the big brown Alaskan husky, while Copper began the injection treatment. The dog was not anxious to cooperate; the needle was painful, and already he'd experienced considerable needle work that morning. Five stitches held closed a slash that ran form his shoulder, across the ribs, halfway down his body. One only fang was broken off short; the missing part was to be found half buried in the shoulder bone of the monstrous thing on the table in the Ad Building.

"How long will that take?" Garry asked, pressing his arm gently. It was sore from the prick of the needle Dr. Copper had used to withdraw blood.

Copper shrugged. "I don't know, to be frank. I know the general method. I've used it on rabbits. But I haven't experimented with dogs. They're big, clumsy animals to work with; naturally rabbits are preferable, and serve ordinarily. In civilized places you can buy a stock of human-immune rabbits from suppliers, and not many investigators take the trouble to prepare their own."

"What do they want with them back there?" Clark asked.

"Criminology is one large field. A says he didn't murder B, but that the blood on his shirt came from killing a chicken. The State makes a test, then it's up to A to explain how it is the blood reacts on human-immune rabbits, but not on chicken-immunes."

"What are we going to do with Blair in the meantime?" Garry asked wearily. "It's all right to let him sleep where he is for a while, but when he wakes up — "

"Barclay and Benning are fitting some bolts on the door of Cosmos House," Copper replied grimly. "Connant's acting like a gentleman. I think perhaps the way the other men look at him makes him rather want privacy. Lord knows, heretofore we've all of us individually prayed for a little privacy."

Clark laughed brittlely. "Not any more, thank you. The more the merrier."

"Blair," Copper went on, "will also have to have privacy — and locks. He's going to have a pretty definite plan in mind when he wakes up. Ever hear the old story of how to stop hoof-and-mouth disease in cattle?"

Clark and Garry shook their heads silently.

"If there isn't any hoof-and-mouth disease, there won't be any hoof-and-mouth disease," Copper explained. "You get rid of it by killing every animal that exhibits it, and every animal that's been near the diseased animal. Blair's a biologist, and knows that story. He's afraid of this thing we loosed. The answer is probably pretty clear in his mind now. Kill everybody and everything in this camp before a skua gull or a wandering albatross coming in with the spring chances out this way and — catches the disease."

Clark's lips curled in a twisted grin. "Sounds logical to me. If things get too bad — maybe we'd better let Blair get loose. It would save us committing suicide. We might also make something of a vow that if things get bad, we see that that does happen."

Copper laughed softly. "The last man alive in Big Magnet — wouldn't be a man," he pointed out. "Somebody's got to kill those — creatures that don't desire to kill themselves, you know. We don't have enough thermite to do it all at once, and the decanite explosive wouldn't help much. I have an idea that even small pieces of one of those beings would be self-sufficient."

"If," said Garry thoughtfully, "they can modify their protoplasm at will, won't they simply modify themselves to birds and fly away? They can read all about birds, and imitate their structure without even meeting them. Or imitate, perhaps, birds of their home planet."

Copper shook his head, and helped Clark to free the dog. "Man studied birds for centuries, trying to learn how to make a machine to fly like them. He never did do the trick; his final success came when he broke away entirely and tried new methods. Knowing the general idea, and knowing the detailed structure of wing and bone and nerve-tissue is something far, far different. And as for other-world birds, perhaps, in fact very probably, the atmospheric conditions here are so vastly different that their birds couldn't fly. Perhaps, even, the being came from a planet like Mars with such a thin atmosphere that there were no birds."

Barclay came into the building, trailing a length of airplane control cable. "It's finished, Doc. Cosmos House can't be opened from the inside. Now where do we put Blair?"

Copper looked toward Garry. "There wasn't any biology building. I don't know where we can isolate him."

"How about East Cache?" Garry said after a moment's thought. "Will Blair be able to look after himself — or need attention?"

"He'll be capable enough. We'll be the ones to watch out," Copper assured him grimly. "Take a stove, a couple of bags of coal, necessary supplies and a few tools to fix it up. Nobody's been out there since last fall, have they?"

Garry shook his head. "If he gets noisy — I thought that might be a good idea."

Barclay hefted the tools he was carrying and looked up at Garry. "If the muttering he's doing now is any sign, he's going to sing away the night hours. And we won't like his song."

"What's he saying?" Copper asked.

Barclay shook his head. "I didn't care to listen much. You can if you want to. But I gathered that the blasted idiot had all the dreams McReady had, and a few more. He slept beside the thing when we stopped on the trail coming in from Secondary Magnetic, remember. He dreamt the thing was alive, and dreamt more details. And — damn his soul — knew it wasn't all dream, or had reason to. He knew it had telepathic powers that were stirring vaguely, and that it could not only read minds, but project thoughts. They weren't dreams, you see. They were stray thoughts that thing was broadcasting, the way Blair's broadcasting his thoughts now — a sort of telepathic muttering in its sleep. That's why he knew so much about its powers. I guess you and I, Doc, weren't so sensitive — if you want to believe in telepathy."

"I have to," Copper sighed. "Dr. Rhine of Duke University has shown that it exists, shown that some are much more sensitive than others."

"Well, if you want to learn a lot of details, go listen in on Blair's broadcast. He's driven most of the boys out of the Ad Building; Kinner's rattling pans like coal going down a chute. When he can't rattle a pan, he shakes ashes.

"By the way, Commander, what are we going to do this spring, now the planes are out of it?"

Garry sighed. "I'm afraid our expedition is going to be a loss. We cannot divide our strength now."

"It won't be a loss — if we continue to live, and come out of this," Copper promised him. "The find we've made, if we can get it under control, is important enough. The cosmic ray data, magnetic work, and atmospheric work won't be greatly hindered."

Garry laughed mirthlessly. "I was just thinking of the radio broadcasts. Telling half the world about the wonderful results of our exploration flights, trying to fool men like Byrd and Ellsworth back home there that we're doing something."

Copper nodded gravely. "They'll know something's wrong. But men like that have judgment enough to know we wouldn't do tricks without some sort of reason, and will wait for our return to judge us. I think it comes to this: men who know enough to recognize our deception will wait for our return. Men who haven't discretion and faith enough to wait will not have the experience to detect any fraud. We know enough of the conditions here to put through a good bluff."

"Just so they don't send 'rescue' expeditions," Garry prayed. "When — if — we're ever ready to come out, we'll have to send

word to Captain Forsythe to bring a stock of
magnetos with him when he comes down.
But — never mind that."

"You mean if we don't come out?" asked
Barclay. "I was wondering if a nice running
account of an eruption or an earthquake via
radio — with a swell windup by using a stick
of decanite under the microphone — would
help. Nothing, of course, will entirely keep
people out. One of those swell, melodramatic
'last-man-alive-scenes' might make 'em go
easy, though."

Garry smiled with genuine humor. "Is everybody in camp trying to figure that out, too?"

Copper laughed. "What do you think, Garry?
We're confident we can win out. But not too
easy about it, I guess."

Clark grinned up from the dog he was
petting into calmness. "Confident, did you
say, Doc?"

8

Blair moved restlessly around the small
shack. His eyes jerked and quivered in vague,
fleeting glances at the four men with him;
Barclay, six feet tall and weighing over 190
pounds; McReady, a bronze giant of a man;
Dr. Copper, short, squatly powerful; and Benning, five feet ten of wiry strength.

Blair was huddled up against the far wall
of the East Cache cabin, his gear piled in the
middle of the floor beside the heating stove,

forming an island between him and the four men. His bony hands clenched and fluttered, terrified. His pale eyes wavered uneasily as his bald, freckled head darted about in bird-like motion.

"I don't want anybody coming here. I'll cook my own food," he snapped nervously. "Kinner may be human now, but I don't believe it. I'm going to get out of here, but I'm not going to eat any food you send me. I want cans. Sealed cans."

"OK, Blair, we'll bring 'em tonight," Barclay promised. "You've got coal, and the fire's started. I'll make a last — " Barclay started forward.

Blair instantly scurried to the farthest corner. "Get out! Keep away from me, you monster!" the little biologist shrieked, and tried to claw his way through the wall of the shack. "Keep away from me — keep away — I won't be absorbed — I won't be — "

Barclay relaxed and moved back. Dr. Copper shook his head. "Leave him alone, Bar. It's easier for him to fix the thing himself. We'll have to fix the door, I think — "

The four men let themselves out. Efficiently, Benning and Barclay fell to work. There were no locks in Antarctica; there wasn't enough privacy to make them needed. But powerful screws had been driven in each side of the door frame, and the spare aviation control cable, immensely strong, woven steel wire, was rapidly caught between them and drawn taut. Barclay went to work with a drill and a

key-hole saw. Presently he had a trap cut in
the door through which goods could be passed
without unlashing the entrance. Three powerful hinges from a stock crate, two hasps and
a pair of three-inch cotter pins made it proof
against opening from the other side.

Blair moved about restlessly inside. He was
dragging something over to the door with
panting gasps, and muttering frantic curses.
Barclay opened the hatch and glanced in, Dr.
Copper peering over his shoulder. Blair had
moved the heavy bunk against the door. It
could not be opened without his cooperation
now.

"Don't know but what the poor man's right
at that," McReady sighed. "If he gets loose, it
is his avowed intention to kill each and all of
us as quickly as possible, which is something
we don't agree with. But we've something on
our side of that door that is worse than a
homicidal maniac. If one or the other has to
get loose, I think I'll come up and undo these
lashings here."

Barclay grinned. "You let me know, and I'll
show you how to get these off fast. Let's go
back."

The sun was painting the northern horizon
in multicolored rainbows still, though it was
two hours below the horizon. The field of drift
swept off to the north, sparkling under its
flaming colors in a million reflected glories.
Low mounds of rounded white on the northern
horizon showed the Magnet Range was barely

awash above the sweeping drift. Little eddies
of wind-lifted snow swirled away from their
skis as they set out toward the main encamp-
ment two miles away. The spidery finger of the
broadcast radiator lifted a gaunt black needle
against the white of the Antarctic continent.
The snow under their skis was like fine sand,
hard and gritty.

"Spring," said Benning bitterly, "is come.
Ain't we got fun! And I've been looking forward to getting away from this blasted hole
in the ice."

"I wouldn't try it now, if I were you." Barclay
grunted. "Guys that set out from here in the
next few days are going to be marvelously
unpopular."

"How is your dog getting along, Dr.
Copper?" McReady asked. "Any results yet?"

"In thirty hours? I wish there were. I gave
him an injection of my blood today. But I
imagine another five days will be needed. I
don't know certainly enough to stop sooner."

"I've been wondering — if Connant were —
changed, would he have warned us so soon
after the animal escaped? Wouldn't he have
waited long enough for it to have a real chance
to fix itself? Until we woke up naturally?"
McReady asked slowly.

"The thing is selfish. You didn't think it
looked as though it were possessed of a store
of the higher justices, did you?" Dr. Copper
pointed out. "Every part of it is all of it, every
part of it is all for itself, I imagine. If Connant

were changed, to save his skin, he'd have to
— but Connant's feelings aren't changed;
they're imitated perfectly, or they're his own.
Naturally, the imitation, imitating perfectly
Connant's feelings, would do exactly what
Connant would do."

"Say, couldn't Norris or Vane give Connant
some kind of a test? If the thing is brighter
than men, it might know more physics than
Connant should, and they'd catch it out,"
Barclay suggested.

Copper shook his head wearily. "Not if it
reads minds. You can't plan a trap for it. Vane
suggested that last night. He hoped it would
answer some of the questions of physics he'd
like to know answers to."

"This expedition-of-four idea is going to
make life happy." Benning looked at his companions. "Each of us with an eye on the other
to make sure he doesn't do something —
peculiar. Man, aren't we going to be a trust-
ing bunch! Each man eyeing his neigbhors
with the grandest exhibition of faith and
trust — I'm beginning to know what Connant
meant by 'I wish you could see your eyes.'
Every now and then we all have it, I guess.
One of you looks around with a sort of 'I-
wonder-if-the-other-*three*-are-look.' Incident-
ally, I'm not excepting myself."

"So far as we know, the animal is dead,
with a slight question as to Connant. No
other is suspected," McReady stated slowly.
"The 'always-four' order is merely a precau-
tionary measure."

"I'm waiting for Garry to make it four-in-a-bunk," Barclay sighed. "I thought I didn't have any privacy before, but since that order — "

9

None watched more tensely than Connant. A little sterile glass test tube, half filled with straw-colored fluid. One — two — three — four — five drops of the clear solution Dr. Copper had prepared from the drops of blood from Connant's arm. The tube was shaken carefully, then set in a beaker of clear, warm water. The thermometer read blood heat, a little thermostat clicked noisily, and the electric hotplate began to glow as the lights flickered slightly. Then — little white flecks of precipitation were forming, snowing down in the clear straw-colored fluid. "Lord," said Connant. He dropped heavily into a bunk, crying like a baby. "Six days — " Connant sobbed, "six days in there — wondering if that damned test would lie — "

Garry moved over silently, and slipped his arm across the physicist's back.

"It couldn't lie," Dr. Copper said. "The dog was human-immune — and the serum reacted."

"He's — all right?" Norris gasped. "Then — the animal is dead — dead forever?"

"He is human," Copper spoke definitely, "and the animal is dead."

Kinner burst out laughing, laughing hysterically. McReady turned toward him and slapped his face with a methodical one-two, one-two action. The cook laughed, gulped, cried a moment, and sat up rubbing his cheeks, mumbling his thanks vaguely. "I was scared. Lord, I was scared — "

Norris laughed brittlely. "You think we weren't, you ape? You think maybe Connant wasn't?"

The Ad Building stirred with a sudden rejuvenation. Voices laughed, the men clustering around Connant spoke with unnecessarily loud voices, jittery, nervous voices relievedly friendly again. Somebody called out a suggestion, and a dozen started for their skis. Blair, Blair might recover — Dr. Copper fussed with his test tubes in nervous relief, trying solutions. The party of relief for Blair's shack started out the door, skis clapping noisily. Down the corridor, the dogs set up a quick yelping howl as the air of excited relief reached them.

Dr. Copper fussed with his tubes. McReady noticed him first, sitting on the edge of the bunk, with two precipitin-whitened test tubes of straw-colored fluid, his face whiter than the stuff in the tubes, silent tears slipping down horror-widened eyes.

McReady felt a cold knife of fear pierce through his heart and freeze in his breast. Dr. Copper looked up. "Garry," he called hoarsely. "Garry, for God's sake, come here."

Commander Garry walked toward him sharply. Silence clapped down on the Ad Building. Connant looked up, rose stiffly from his seat.

"Garry — tissue from the monster — precipitates, too. It proves nothing. Nothing but — but the dog was monster-immune too. That *one of the two contributing blood — one of us two,* you and I, Garry — *one of us is a monster.*"

10

"Bar, call back those men before they tell Blair," McReady said quietly. Barclay went to the door; faintly his shouts came back to the tensely silent men in the room. Then he was back.

"They're coming," he said. "I didn't tell them why. Just that Dr. Copper said not to go."

"McReady," Garry sighed, "you're in command now. May God help you. I cannot."

The bronzed giant nodded slowly, his deep eyes on Commander Garry.

"I may be the one," Garry added. "I know I'm not, but I cannot prove it to you in any way. Dr. Copper's test has broken down. The fact that he showed it was useless, when it was to the advantage of the monster to have that uselessness not known, would seem to prove he was human."

Copper rocked back and forth slowly on the bunk. "I know I'm human. I can't prove it either. One of us two is a liar, for that test cannot lie, and it says one of us is. I gave proof that the test was wrong, which seems to prove I'm human, and now Garry has given that argument which proves me human — which he, as the monster, should not do. Round and round and round and round and — "

Dr. Copper's head, then his neck and shoulders began circling slowly in time to the words. Suddenly he was lying back on the bunk, roaring with laughter. "It doesn't have to prove *one* of us is a monster! It doesn't have to prove that at all! Ho-ho. If we're *all* monsters it works the same — we're all monsters — all of us — Connant and Garry and I — and all of you."

"McReady," Van Wall, the blond-bearded Chief Pilot, called softly, "you were on the way to an M.D. when you took up meteorology, weren't you? Can you make some kind of test?"

McReady went over to Copper slowly, took the hypodermic from his hand, and washed it carefully in ninety-five percent alcohol. Garry sat on the bunk edge with wooden face, watching Copper and McReady expressionlessly. "What Copper said is possible," McReady sighed. "Van, will you help here? Thanks." The filled needle jabbed into Copper's thigh. The man's laughter did not stop, but slowly faded into sobs, then sound sleep as the morphia took hold.

McReady turned again. The men who had started for Blair stood at the far end of the room, skis dripping snow, their faces as white as their skis. Connant had a lighted cigarette in each hand; one he was puffing absently, and staring at the floor. The heat of the one in his left hand attracted him and he stared at it and the one in the other hand stupidly for a moment. He dropped one and crushed it under his heel slowly.

"Dr. Copper," McReady repeated, "could be right. I know I'm human — but of course can't prove it. I'll repeat the test for my own information. Any of you others who wish to may do the same."

Two minutes later, McReady held a test tube with white precipitin settling slowly from straw-colored serum. "It reacts to human blood too, so they aren't both monsters."

"I didn't think they were," Van Wall sighed. "That wouldn't suit the monster either; we could have destroyed them if we knew. Why hasn't the monster destroyed us, do you suppose? It seems to be loose."

McReady snorted. Then laughed softly. "Elementary, my dear Watson. The monster wants to have life-forms available. It cannot animate a dead body, apparently. It is just waiting — waiting until the best opportunities come. We who remain human, it is holding in reserve."

Kinner shuddered violently. "Hey. Hey, Mac. Mac, would I know if I was a monster? Would I know if the monster had already got me? Oh Lord, I may be a monster already."

"You'd know," McReady answered.

"But we wouldn't," Norris laughed shortly, half hysterically.

McReady looked at the vial of serum remaining. "There's one thing this damned stuff is good for, at that," he said thoughtfully. "Clark, will you and Van help me? The rest of the gang better stick together here. Keep an eye on each other," he said bitterly. "See that you don't get into mischief, shall we say?"

McReady started down the tunnel toward Dogtown, with Clark and Van Wall behind him. "You need more serum?" Clark asked.

McReady shook his head. "Tests. There's four cows and a bull, and nearly seventy dogs down there. This stuff reacts only to human blood and — monsters."

11

McReady came back to the Ad Building and went silently to the wash stand. Clark and Van Wall joined him a moment later. Clark's lips had developed a tic, jerking into sudden, unexpected sneers.

"What did you do?" Connant exploded suddenly. "More immunizing?"

Clark snickered, and stopped with a hiccough. "Immunizing. Haw! Immune all right."

"That monster," said Van Wall steadily, "is quite logical. Our immune dog was quite all right, and we drew a little more serum for the tests. But we won't make any more."

"Can't — can't you use one man's blood on another dog — " Norris began.

"There aren't," said McReady softly, "any more dogs. Nor cattle, I might add."

"No more dogs?" Benning sat down slowly.

"They're very nasty when they start changing," Van Wall said precisely. "But slow. That electrocution iron you made up, Barclay, is very fast. There is only one dog left — our immune. The monster left that for us, so we could play with our little test. The rest — " He shrugged and dried his hands.

"The cattle — " gulped Kinner.

"Also. Reacted very nicely. They look funny as hell when they start melting. The beast hasn't any quick escape, when it's tied in dog chains, or halters, and it had to be to imitate."

Kinner stood up slowly. His eyes darted around the room, and came to rest horribly quivering on a tin bucket in the galley. Slowly, step by step he retreated toward the door, his mouth opening and closing silently, like a fish out of water.

"The milk — " he gasped. "I milked 'em an hour ago — " His voice broke into a scream as he dived through the door. He was out on the ice cap without windproof or heavy clothing.

Van Wall looked after him for a moment thoughtfully. "He's probably hopelessly mad," he said at length, "but he might be a monster escaping. He hasn't skis. Take a blowtorch — in case."

The physical motion of the chase helped

them; something that needed doing. Three of the other men were quietly being sick. Norris was lying flat on his back, his face greenish, looking steadily at the bottom of the bunk above him.

"Mac, how long have the — cows been not-cows — "

McReady shrugged his shoulders hopelessly. He went over to the milk bucket, and with his little tube of serum went to work on it. The milk clouded it, making certainty difficult. Finally he dropped the test tube in the stand, and shook his head. "It tests negatively. Which means either they were cows then, or that, being perfect imitations, they gave perfectly good milk."

Copper stirred restlessly in his sleep and gave a gurgling cross between a snore and a laugh. Silent eyes fastened on him. "Would morphia — a monster — " somebody started to ask.

"Lord knows," McReady shrugged. "It affects every Earthly animal I know of."

Connant suddenly raised his head. "Mac! The dogs must have swallowed pieces of the monster, and the pieces destroyed them! The dogs were where the monster resided. I was locked up. Doesn't that prove — "

Van Wall shook his head. "Sorry. Proves nothing about what you are, only proves what you didn't do."

"It doesn't do that," McReady sighed. "We are helpless because we don't know enough, and so jittery we don't think straight. Locked up! Ever watch a white corpuscle of the blood go through the wall of a blood vessel? No? It sticks out a pseudopod. And there it is — on the far side of the wall."

"Oh," said Van Wall unhappily. "The cattle tried to melt down, didn't they? They could have melted down — become just a thread of stuff and leaked under a door to re-collect on the other side. Ropes — no — no, that wouldn't do it. They couldn't live in a sealed tank or — "

"If," said McReady, "you shoot it through the heart, and it doesn't die, it's a monster. That's the best test I can think of, offhand."

"No dogs," said Garry quietly, "and no cattle. It has to imitate men now. And locking up doesn't do any good. Your test might work, Mac, but I'm afraid it would be hard on the men."

12

Clark looked up from the galley stove as Van Wall, Barclay, McReady, and Benning came in, brushing the drift from their clothes. The other men jammed into the Ad Building continued studiously to do as they were doing, playing chess, poker, reading. Ralsen was fixing a sledge on the table; Vane and Norris had their heads together over magnetic data, while Harvey read tables in a low voice.

Dr. Copper snored softly on the bunk. Garry was working with Dutton over a sheaf of radio messages on the corner of Dutton's bunk and a small fraction of the radio table. Connant was using most of the table for cosmic ray sheets.

Quite plainly through the corridor, despite two closed doors, they could hear Kinner's voice. Clark banged a kettle onto the galley stove and beckoned McReady silently. The meteorologist went over to him.

"I don't mind the cooking so damn much," Clark said nervously, "but isn't there some way to stop that bird? We all agreed that it would be safe to move him into Cosmos House."

"Kinner?" McReady nodded toward the door. "I'm afraid not. I can dope him, I suppose, but we don't have an unlimited supply of morphia, and he's not in danger of losing his mind. Just hysterical."

"Well, we're in danger of losing ours. You've been out for an hour and a half. That's been going on steadily ever since, and it was going for two hours before. There's a limit, you know."

Garry wandered over slowly, apologetically. For an instant, McReady caught the feral spark of fear — horror — in Clark's eyes, and knew at the same instant it was in his own. Garry — Garry or Copper — was certainly a monster.

"If you could stop that, I think it would be a sound policy, Mac," Garry spoke quietly.

"There are — tensions enough in this room. We agreed that it would be safe for Kinner in there, because everyone else in camp is under constant eyeing." Garry shivered slightly. "And try, try in God's name, to find some test that will work."

McReady sighed. "Watched or unwatched, everyone's tense. Blair's jammed the trap so it won't open now. Says he's got food enough, and keeps screaming 'Go away, go away — you're monsters. I won't be absorbed. I won't. I'll tell men when they come. Go away.' So — we went away."

"There's no other test?" Garry pleaded.

McReady shrugged his shoulders. "Copper was perfectly right. The serum test could be absolutely definitive if it hadn't been — contaminated. But that's the only dog left, and he's fixed now."

"Chemicals? Chemical tests?"

McReady shook his head. "Our chemistry isn't that good. I tried the microscope you know."

Garry nodded. "Monster-dog and real dog were identical. But — you've got to go on. What are we going to do after dinner?"

Van Wall had joined them quietly. "Rotation sleeping. Half the crowd sleep; half stay awake. I wonder how many of us are monsters? All the dogs were. We thought we were safe, but somehow it got Copper — or you." Van Wall's eyes flashed uneasily. "It may have gotten every one of you — all of you but myself may be wondering, looking. No, that's not possible. You'd just spring then, I'd be helpless. We humans must somehow have the greater numbers now. But — " he stopped.

McReady laughed shortly. "You're doing what Norris complained of in me. Leaving it hanging. 'But if one more is changed — that may shift the balance of power.' It doesn't fight. I don't think it ever fights. It must be a peaceable thing, in its own — inimitable — way. It never had to, because it always gained its end otherwise."

Van Wall's mouth twisted in a sickly grin. "You're suggesting then, that perhaps it already *has* the greater numbers, but is just waiting — waiting, all of them — all of you, for all I know — waiting till I, the last human, drop my wariness in sleep. Mac, did you notice their eyes, all looking at us."

Garry sighed. "You haven't been sitting here for four straight hours, while all their eyes silently weighed the information that one of us two, Copper or I, is a monster certainly — perhaps both of us."

Clark repeated his request. "Will you stop that bird's noise? He's driving me nuts. Make him tone down, anyway."

"Still praying?" McReady asked.

"Still praying," Clark groaned. "He hasn't stopped for a second. I don't mind his praying if it relieves him, but he yells, he sings psalms and hymns and shouts prayers. He thinks God can't hear well way down here."

"Maybe he can't," Barclay grunted. "Or he'd

have done something about this thing loosed from hell."

"Somebody's going to try that test you mentioned, if you don't stop him," Clark stated grimly. "I think a cleaver in the head would be as positive a test as a bullet in the heart."

"Go ahead with the food. I'll see what I can do. There may be something in the cabinets." McReady moved wearily toward the corner Copper had used as his dispensary. Three tall cabinets of rough boards, two locked, were the repositories of the camp's medical supplies. Twelve years ago, McReady had graduated, had started for an internship, and been diverted to meteorology. Copper was a picked man, a man who knew his profession thoroughly and modernly. More than half the drugs available were totally unfamiliar to McReady; many of the others he had forgotten. There was no huge medical library here, no series of journals available to learn the things he had forgotten, the elementary, simple things to Copper, things that did not merit inclusion in the small library he had been forced to content himself with. Books are heavy, and every ounce of supplies had been freighted in by air.

McReady picked a barbiturate hopefully. Barclay and Van Wall went with him. One man never went anywhere alone in Big Magnet.

Ralsen had his sledge put away, and the physicists had moved off the table, the poker game broken up when they got back. Clark was putting out the food. The click of spoons and the muffled sounds of eating were the only sign of life in the room. There were no words spoken as the three returned; simply all eyes focused on them questioningly while the jaws moved methodically.

McReady stiffened suddenly. Kinner was screeching out a hymn in a hoarse, cracked voice. He looked wearily at Van Wall with a twisted grin and shook his head. "Uh-uh."

Van Wall cursed bitterly, and sat down at the table. "We'll just plumb have to take that till his voice wears out. He can't yell like that forever."

"He's got a brass throat and a cast-iron larynx," Norris declared savagely. "Then we could be hopeful, and suggest he's one of our friends. In that case he could go on renewing his throat till doomsday."

Silence clamped down. For twenty minutes they ate without a word. Then Connant jumped up with an angry violence. "You sit as still as a bunch of graven images. You don't say a word, but oh, Lord, what expressive eyes you've got. They roll around like a bunch of glass marbles spilling down a table. They wink and blink and stare — and whisper things. Can you guys look somewhere else for a change, please?

"Listen, Mac, you're in charge here. Let's run movies for the rest of the night. We've been saving those reels to make 'em last. Last for what? Who is it's going to see those last reels, eh? Let's see 'em while we can, and look at something other than each other."

"Sound idea, Connant. I, for one, am quite willing to change this in any way I can."

"Turn the sound up loud, Dutton. Maybe you can drown out the hymns," Clark suggested.

"But don't," Norris said softly, "don't turn off the lights altogether."

"The lights will be out." McReady shook his head. "We'll show all the cartoon movies we have. You won't mind seeing the old cartoons will you?"

"Goody, goody — a moom-pitcher show. I'm just in the mood." McReady turned to look at the speaker, a lean, lanky New Englander, by the name of Caldwell. Caldwell was stuffing his pipe slowly, a sour eye cocked up to McReady.

The bronze giant was forced to laugh. "OK, Bart, you win. Maybe we aren't quite in the mood for Popeye and trick ducks, but it's something."

"Let's play Classifications," Caldwell suggested slowly. "Or maybe you call it Guggenheim. You draw lines on a piece of paper, and put down classes of things — like animals, you know. One for 'H' and one for 'U' and so on. Like 'Human' and 'Unknown' for instance. I think that would be a hell of a lot better game. Classification, I sort of figure, is what we need right now a lot more than movies. Maybe somebody's got a pencil that he can draw lines with, draw lines between the 'U' animals and the 'H' animals for instance."

"McReady's trying to find that kind of pencil," Van Wall answered quietly, "but, we've got three kinds of animals here, you know. One that begins with 'M.' We don't want any more."

"Mad ones, you mean. Uh-huh. Clark, I'll help you with those pots so we can get our little peep show going." Caldwell got up slowly.

Dutton and Barclay and Benning, in charge of the projector and sound mechanism arrangements, went about their job silently, while the Ad Building was cleared and the dishes and pans disposed of. McReady drifted over toward Van Wall slowly, and leaned back in the bunk beside him. "I've been wondering, Van," he said with a wry grin, "whether or not to report my ideas in advance. I forgot the 'U animal' as Caldwell named it, could read minds. I've a vague idea of something that might work. It's too vague to bother with, though. Go ahead with your show, while I try to figure out the logic of the thing. I'll take this bunk."

Van Wall glanced up, and nodded. The movie screen would be practically on a line with this bunk, hence making the pictures least distracting here, because least intelligible. "Perhaps you should tell us what you have in mind. As it is, only the unknowns know what you plan. You might be — unknown before you got it into operation."

"Won't take long, if I get it figured out

right. But I don't want any more all-but-the-test-dog-monsters things. We better move Copper into this bunk directly above me. He won't be watching the screen either." McReady nodded toward Copper's gently snoring bulk. Garry helped them lift and move the doctor.

McReady leaned back against the bunk, and sank into a trance, almost, of concentration, trying to calculate chances, operations, methods. He was scarcely aware as the others distributed themselves silently, and the screen lit up. Vaguely Kinner's hectic, shouted prayers and his rasping hymn-singing annoyed him till the sound accompaniment started. The lights were turned out, but the large, light-colored areas of the screen reflected enough light for ready visibility. It made men's eyes sparkle as they moved restlessly. Kinner was still praying, shouting, his voice a raucous accompaniment to the mechanical sound. Dutton stepped up the amplification.

So long had the voice been going on, that only vaguely at first was McReady aware that something seemed missing. Lying as he was, just across the narrow room from the corridor leading to Cosmos House, Kinner's voice had reached him fairly clearly, despite the sound accompaniment of the pictures. It struck him abruptly that it had stopped.

"Dutton, cut that sound," McReady called as he sat up abruptly. The pictures flickered a moment, soundless and strangely futile in the sudden, deep silence. The rising wind on the surface above bubbled melancholy tears of sound down the stove pipes. "Kinner's stopped," McReady said softly.

"For God's sake start that sound then; he may have stopped to listen," Norris snapped.

McReady rose and went down the corridor. Barclay and Van Wall left their places at the far end of the room to follow him. The flickers bulged and twisted on the back of Barclay's gray underwear as he crossed the still-functioning beam of the projector. Dutton snapped on the lights, and the picture vanished.

Norris stood at the door as McReady had asked. Garry sat down quietly in the bunk nearest the door, forcing Clark to make room for him. Most of the others had stayed exactly where they were. Only Connant walked slowly up and down the room, in steady, unvarying rhythm.

"If you're going to do that, Connant," Clark spat, "we can get along without you altogether, whether you're human or not. Will you stop that damned rhythm?"

"Sorry." The physicist sat down in a bunk, and watched his toes thoughtfully. It was almost five minutes, five ages, while the wind made the only sound, before McReady appeared at the door.

"We," he announced, "haven't got enough grief here already. Somebody's tried to help us out. Kinner has a knife in his throat, which was why he stopped singing, probably. We've got monsters, madmen, and murderers. Any more 'M's' you can think of, Caldwell? If there are, we'll probably have 'em before long."

13

"Is Blair loose?" someone asked.

"Blair is not loose. Or he flew in. If there's any doubt about where our gentle helper came from — this may clear it up." Van Wall held a foot-long, thin-bladed knife in a cloth. The wooden handle was half burnt, charred with the peculiar pattern of the top of the galley stove.

Clark stared at it. "I did that this after-noon. I forgot the damn thing and left it on the stove."

Van Wall nodded. "I smelled it, if you re-member. I knew the knife came from the galley."

"I wonder," said Benning looking around at the party warily, "how many more monsters have we? If somebody could slip out of his place, go back of the screen to the galley, and then down to the Cosmos House and back — he did come back didn't he? Yes — every-body's here. Well, if one of the gang could do all that — "

"Maybe a monster did it," Garry suggested quietly. "There's that possibility."

"The monster, as you pointed out today, has

only men left to imitate. Would he decrease
his — supply, shall we say?" Van Wall pointed
out. "No, we just have a plain, ordinary louse,
a murderer to deal with. Ordinarily we'd call
him an 'inhuman murderer' I suppose, but we
have to distinguish now. We have inhuman
murderers, and now we have human murderers. Or one at least."

"There's one less human," Norris said
softly. "Maybe the monsters have the balance
of power now."

"Never mind that," McReady sighed and
turned to Barclay. "Bar, will you get your
electric gadget? I'm going to make certain — "

Barclay turned down the corridor to get the
pronged electrocuter, while McReady and Van
Wall went back toward Cosmos House. Barclay followed them in some thirty seconds.

The corridor to Cosmos House twisted, as
did nearly all corridors in Big Magnet, and
Norris stood at the entrance again. But they
heard, rather muffled, McReady's sudden
shout. There was a savage flurry of blows,
dull *ch-thunk, shluff* sounds. "Bar — Bar — "
And a curious, savage mewing scream,
silenced before even quick-moving Norris had
reached the bend.

Kinner — or what had been Kinner — lay
on the floor, cut half in two by the great
knife McReady had had. The meteorologist
stood against the wall, the knife dripping red
in his hand. Van Wall was stirring vaguely on
the floor, moaning, his hand half-consciously
rubbing at his jaw. Barclay, an unutterably

savage gleam in his eyes, was methodically leaning on the pronged weapon in his hand, jabbing — jabbing, jabbing.

Kinner's arms had developed a queer, scaly fur, and the flesh had twisted. The fingers had shortened, the hand rounded, the fingernails become three-inch long things of dull red horn, keened to steel-hard, razor-sharp talons.

McReady raised his head, looked at the knife in his hand and dropped it. "Well, whoever did it can speak up now. He was an inhuman murderer at that — in that he murdered an inhuman. I swear by all that's holy, Kinner was a lifeless corpse on the floor here when we arrived. But when It found we were going to jab It with the power — It changed."

Norris stared unsteadily. "Oh, Lord, those things can act. Ye gods — sitting in here for hours, mouthing prayers to a God it hated! Shouting hymns in a cracked voice — hymns about a Church it never knew. Driving us mad with its ceaseless howling —

"Well. Speak up, whoever did it. You didn't know it, but you did the camp a favor. And I want to know how in blazes you got out of the room without anyone seeing you. It might help in guarding ourselves."

"His screaming — his singing. Even the sound projector couldn't drown it." Clark shivered. "It was a monster."

"Oh," said Van Wall in sudden comprehension. "You *were* sitting right next to the door, weren't you? And almost behind the projection screen already."

Clark nodded dumbly. "He — it's quiet now. It's a dead — Mac, your test's no damn good. It was dead anyway, monster or man, it was dead."

McReady chuckled softly. "Boys, meet Clark, the only one we know is human! Meet Clark, the one who proves he's human by trying to commit murder — and failing. Will the rest of you please refrain from trying to prove you're human for a while? I think we may have another test."

"A test!" Connant snapped joyfully, then his face sagged in disappointment. "I suppose it's another either-way-you-want-it."

"No," said McReady steadily. "Look sharp and be careful. Come into the Ad Building. Barclay, bring your electrocuter. And somebody — Dutton — stand with Barclay to make sure he does it. Watch every neighbor, for by the Hell these monsters came from, I've got something, and they know it. They're going to get dangerous!"

The group tensed abruptly. An air of crushing menace entered into every man's body, sharply they looked at each other. More keenly than ever before — *is that man next to me an inhuman monster?*

"What is it?" Garry asked, as they stood again in the main room. "How long will it take?"

"I don't know, exactly," said McReady, his voice brittle with angry determination. "But I *know* it will work, and no two ways about it. It depends on a basic quality of the *monsters,* not on us. *'Kinner'* just convinced me." He stood heavy and solid in bronzed immobility, completely sure of himself again at last.

"This," said Barclay, hefting the wooden-handled weapon tipped with its two sharp-pointed, charged conductors, "is going to be rather necessary, I take it. Is the power plant assured?"

Dutton nodded sharply. "The automatic stoker bin is full. The gas power plant is on standby. Van Wall and I set it for the movie operation — and we've checked it over rather carefully several times, you know. Anything those wires touch, dies," he assured them grimly. "*I* know that."

Dr. Copper stirred vaguely in his bunk, rubbed his eyes with fumbling hand. He sat up slowly, blinked his eyes blurred with sleep and drugs, widened with an unutterable horror of drug-ridden nightmares. "Garry," he mumbled, "Garry — listen. Selfish — from hell they came, and hellish shellfish — I mean self — Do I? What do I mean?" He sank back in his bunk, and snored softly.

McReady looked at him thoughtfully. "We'll know presently," he nodded slowly. "But selfish is what you mean, all right. You may have thought of that, half sleeping, dreaming there. I didn't stop to think what dreams you might be having. But that's all right. Selfish is the word. They must be, you see." He turned to the men in the cabin, tense, silent men staring with wolfish eyes each at his neighbor. "Selfish, and as Dr. Copper said —

every part is a whole. Every piece is self-
sufficient, an animal in itself.

"That, and one other thing, tell the story.
There's nothing mysterious about blood; it's
just as normal a body tissue as a piece of
muscle, or a piece of liver. But it hasn't so
much connective tissue, though it has millions, billions of life-cells."

McReady's great bronze beard ruffled in a
grim smile. "This is satisfying, in a way. I'm
pretty sure we humans still outnumber you —
others. Others standing here. And we have
what you, your other-world race, evidently
doesn't. Not an imitated, but a bred-in-the-
bone instinct, a driving, unquenchable fire
that's genuine. We'll fight, fight with a ferocity
you may attempt to imitate, but you'll never
equal! We're human. We're real. You're imitations, false to the core of your every cell.

"All right. It's a showdown now. *You* know.
You, with your mind reading. You've lifted the
idea from my brain. You can't do a thing about
it.

"Standing here —

"Let it pass. Blood is tissue. They have to
bleed; if they don't bleed when cut, then by
Heaven, they're phoney from hell! If they
bleed — then that blood, separated from them,
is an individual — *a newly formed individual
in its own right, just as they — split, all of
them, from one original — are individuals!*

"Get it, Van? See the answer, Bar?"

Van Wall laughed very softly. "The blood —
the blood will not obey. It's a new individual,

with all the desire to protect its own life that the original — the main mass from which it was split — has. The *blood* will live — and try to crawl away from a hot needle, say!"

McReady picked up the scalpel from the table. From the cabinet, he took a rack of test tubes, a tiny alcohol lamp, and a length of platinum wire set in a little glass rod. A smile of grim satisfaction rode his lips. For a moment he glanced up at those around him. Barclay and Dutton moved toward him slowly, the wooden-handled electric instrument alert.

"Dutton," said McReady, "suppose you stand over by the splice there where you've connected that in. Just make sure no — thing pulls it loose."

Dutton moved away. "Now, Van, suppose you be first on this."

White-faced, Van Wall stepped forward. With a delicate precision, McReady cut a vein in the base of his thumb. Van Wall winced slightly, then held steady as a half inch of bright blood collected in the tube. McReady put the tube in the rack, gave Van Wall a bit of alum, and indicated the iodine bottle.

Van Wall stood motionlessly watching. McReady heated the platinum wire in the alcohol lamp flame, then dipped it into the tube. It hissed softly. Five times he repeated the test. "Human, I'd say," McReady sighed, and straightened. "As yet, my theory hasn't been actually proven — but I have hopes. I have hopes.

"Don't, by the way, get too interested in

this. We have with us some unwelcome ones, no doubt. Van, will you relieve Barclay at the switch? Thanks. OK, Barclay, and may I say I hope you stay with us? You're a damned good guy."

Barclay grinned uncertainly; winced under the keen edge of the scalpel. Presently, smiling widely, he retrieved his long-handled weapon.

"Mr. Samuel Dutt — *Bar!*"

The tensity was released in that second. Whatever of hell the monsters may have had within them, the men in that instant matched it. Barclay had no chance to move his weapon, as a score of men poured down on the thing that had seemed Dutton. It mewed, and spat, and tried to grow fangs — and was a hundred broken, torn pieces. Without knives, or any weapon save the brute-given strength of a staff of picked men, the thing was crushed, rent.

Slowly they picked themselves up, their eyes smouldering, very quiet in their motions. A curious wrinkling of their lips betrayed a species of nervousness.

Barclay went over with the electric weapon. Things smouldered and stank. The caustic acid Van Wall dropped on each spilled drop of blood gave off tickling, cough-provoking fumes.

McReady grinned, his deepset eyes alight and dancing. "Maybe," he said softly, "I underrated man's abilities when I said nothing human could have the ferocity in the eyes of

that thing we found. I wish we could have
the opportunity to treat in a more befitting
manner these things. Something with boiling
oil, or melted lead in it, or maybe slow roasting in the power boiler. When I think what a
man Dutton was —

"Never mind. My theory is confirmed by —
by one who knew? Well, Van Wall and Barclay
are proven. I think, then, that I'll try to show
you what I already know. That I, too, am
human." McReady swished the scalpel in absolute alcohol, burned it off the metal blade,
and cut the base of his thumb expertly.

Twenty seconds later he looked up from the
desk at the waiting men. There were more
grins out there now, friendly grins, yet withal,
something else in the eyes.

"Connant," McReady laughed softly, "was
right. The huskies watching that thing in the
corridor bend had nothing on you. Wonder why
we think only the wolf blood has the right to
ferocity? Maybe on spontaneous viciousness
a wolf takes tops, but after these seven days
— abandon all hope, ye wolves who enter
here!

"Maybe we can save time. Connant, would
you step for — "

Again Barclay was too slow. There were
more grins, less tensity still, when Barclay
and Van Wall finished their work.

Garry spoke in a low, bitter voice. "Connant was one of the finest men we had here
— and five minutes ago I'd have sworn he was
a man. Those damnable things are more than

imitation." Garry shuddered and sat back in his bunk.

And thirty seconds later, Garry's blood shrank from the hot platinum wire, and struggled to escape the tube, struggled as frantically as a suddenly feral, red-eyed, dissolving imitation of Garry struggled to dodge the snake-tongue weapon Barclay advanced at him, white-faced and sweating. The Thing in the test tube screamed with a tiny, tinny voice as McReady dropped it into the glowing coal of the galley stove.

14

"The last of it?" Dr. Copper looked down from his bunk with bloodshot, saddened eyes. "Fourteen of them — "

McReady nodded shortly. "In some ways — if only we could have permanently prevented their spreading — I'd like to have even the imitations back. Commander Garry — Connant — Dutton — Clark — "

"Where are they taking those things?" Copper nodded to the stretcher Barclay and Norris were carrying out.

"Outside. Outside on the ice, where they've got fifteen smashed crates, half a ton of coal, and presently will add ten gallons of kerosene. We've dumped acid on every spilled drop, every torn fragment. We're going to incinerate those."

"Sounds like a good plan." Copper nodded

wearily. "I wonder, you haven't said whether Blair — "

McReady started. "We forgot him? We had so much else! I wonder — do you suppose we can cure him now?"

"If — " began Dr. Copper, and stopped meaningly.

McReady started a second time. "Even a madman. It imitated Kinner and his praying hysteria — " McReady turned toward Van Wall at the long table. "Van, we've got to make an expedition to Blair's shack."

Van looked up sharply, the frown of worry faded for an instant in surprised remembrance. Then he rose, nodded. "Barclay better go along. He applied the lashings, and may figure how to get in without frightening Blair too much."

Three quarters of an hour, through —37° cold, while the aurora curtain bellied overhead. The twilight was nearly twelve hours long, flaming in the north on snow like white, crystalline sand under their skis. A five-mile wind piled it in drift-lines pointing off to the northwest. Three quarters of an hour to reach the snow-buried shack. No smoke came from the little shack, and the men hastened.

"Blair!" Barclay roared into the wind when he was still a hundred yards away. "Blair!"

"Shut up," said McReady softly. "And hurry. He may be trying a lone hike. If we have to go after him — no planes, the tractors disabled — "

"Would a monster have the stamina a man has?"

"A broken leg wouldn't stop it for more than a minute," McReady pointed out.

Barclay gasped suddenly and pointed aloft. Dim in the twilit sky, a winged thing circled in curves of indescribable grace and ease. Great white wings tipped gently, and the bird swept over them in silent curiosity. "Albatross — " Barclay said softly. "First of the season, and wandering way inland for some reason. If a monster's loose — "

Norris bent down on the ice, and tore hurriedly at his heavy, windproof clothing. He straightened, his coat flapping open, a grim blue-metaled weapon in his hand. It roared a challenge to the white silence of Antarctica.

The thing in the air screamed hoarsely. Its great wings worked frantically as a dozen feathers floated down from its tail. Norris fired again. The bird was moving swiftly now, but in an almost straight line of retreat. It screamed again, more feathers dropped, and with beating wings it soared behind a ridge of pressure ice, to vanish.

Norris hurried after the others. "It won't come back," he panted.

Barclay cautioned him to silence, pointing. A curiously, fiercely blue light beat out from the cracks of the shack's door. A very low, soft humming sounded inside, a low, soft humming and a clink and click of tools, the very sounds somehow bearing a message of frantic haste.

McReady's face paled. "Lord help us if that thing has — " He grabbed Barclay's shoulder, and made snipping motions with his fingers, pointing toward the lacing of control cables that held the door.

Barclay drew the wire cutters from his pocket, and kneeled soundlessly at the door. The snap and twang of cut wires made an unbearable racket in the utter quiet of the Antarctic hush. There was only that strange, sweetly soft hum from within the shack, and the queerly, hectically clipped clicking and rattling of tools to drown their noises.

McReady peered through a crack in the door. His breath sucked in huskily and his great fingers clamped cruelly on Barclay's shoulder. The meteorologist backed down. "It isn't," he explained very softly, "Blair. It's kneeling on something on the bunk — something that keeps lifting. Whatever it's working on is a thing like a knapsack — and it lifts."

"All at once," Barclay said grimly. "No. Norris, hang back, and get that iron of yours out. It may have — weapons."

Together, Barclay's powerful body and McReady's giant strength struck the door. Inside, the bunk jammed against the door screeched madly and crackled into kindling. The door flung down from broken hinges, the patched lumber of the doorpost dropping inward.

Like a blue rubber ball, a Thing bounced up. One of its four tentacle-like arms looped out like a striking snake. In a seven-tentacled hand a six-inch pencil of winking, shining metal glinted and swung upward to face them. Its line-thin lips twitched back from snake-fangs in a grin of hate, red eyes blazing.

Norris' revolver thundered in the confined space. The hate-washed face twitched in agony, the looping tentacle snatched back. The silvery thing in its hand a smashed ruin of metal, the seven-tentacled hand became a mass of mangled flesh oozing greenish-yellow ichor. The revolver thundered three times more. Dark holes drilled each of the three eyes before Norris hurled the empty weapon against its face.

The Thing screamed in feral hate, a lashing tentacle wiping at blinded eyes. For a moment it crawled on the floor, savage tentacles lashing out, the body twitching. Then it staggered up again, blinded eyes working, boiling hideously, the crushed flesh sloughing away in sodden gobbets.

Barclay lurched to his feet and dove forward with an ice-ax. The flat of the weighty thing crushed against the side of the head. Again the unkillable monster went down. The tentacles lashed out, and suddenly Barclay fell to his feet in the grip of a living, livid rope. The thing dissolved as he held it, a white-hot band that ate into the flesh of his hands like living fire. Frantically he tore the stuff from him, held his hands where they could not be reached. The blind Thing felt and ripped at the tough, heavy, windproof cloth, seeking flesh — flesh it could convert —

The huge blowtorch McReady had brought coughed solemnly. Abruptly it rumbled disapproval throatily. Then it laughed gurglingly, and thrust out a blue-white, three-foot tongue. The Thing on the floor shrieked, flailed out blindly with tentacles that writhed and withered in the bubbling wrath of the blowtorch. It crawled and turned on the floor, it shrieked and hobbled madly, but always McReady held the blowtorch on the face, the dead eyes burning and bubbling uselessly. Frantically the Thing crawled and howled.

A tentacle sprouted a savage talon — and crisped in the flame. Steadily McReady moved with a planned, grim campaign. Helpless, maddened, the Thing retreated from the grunting torch, the caressing, licking tongue. For a moment it rebelled, squalling in inhuman hatred at the touch of the icy snow. Then it fell back before the charring breath of the torch, the stench of its flesh bathing it. Hopelessly it retreated — on and on across the Antarctic snow. The bitter wind swept over it, twisting the torch-tongue; vainly it flopped, a trail of oily, stinking smoke bubbling away from it —

McReady walked back toward the shack silently. Barclay met him at the door. "No more?" the giant meteorologist asked grimly.

Barclay shook his head. "No more. It didn't split?"

"It had other things to think about," McReady assured him. "When I left it, it was a glowing coal. What was it doing?"

Norris laughed shortly. "Wise boys, we are.

Smash magnetos, so planes won't work. Rip
the boiler tubing out of the tractors. And leave
that Thing alone for a week in this shack.
Alone and undisturbed."

McReady looked in at the shack more carefully. The air, despite the ripped door, was
hot and humid. On a table at the far end of
the room rested a thing of coiled wires and
small magnets, glass tubing and radio tubes.
At the center a block of rough stone rested.
From the center of the block came the light
that flooded the place, the fiercely blue light
bluer than the glare of an electric arc, and from
it came the sweetly soft hum. Off to one side
was another mechanism of crystal glass,
blown with an incredible neatness and
delicacy, metal plates and a queer, shimmery
sphere of insubstantiality.

"What is that?" McReady moved nearer.

Norris grunted. "Leave it for investigation.
But I can guess pretty well. That's atomic
power. That stuff to the left — that's a neat
little thing for doing what men have been
trying to do with hundred-ton cyclotrons and
so forth. It separates neutrons from heavy
water, which he was getting from the surrounding ice."

"Where did he get all — oh. Of course. A
monster couldn't be locked in — or out. He's
been through the apparatus caches." McReady
stared at the apparatus. "Lord, what minds
that race must have — "

"The shimmery sphere — I think it's a
sphere of pure force. Neutrons can pass

through any matter, and he wanted a supply reservoir of neutrons. Just project neutrons against silica, calcium, beryllium — almost anything, and the atomic energy is released. That thing is the atomic generator."

McReady plucked a thermometer from his coat. "It's 120° in here, despite the open door. Our clothes have kept the heat out to an extent, but I'm sweating now."

Norris nodded. "The light's cold. I found that. But it gives off heat to warm the place through that coil. He had all the power in the world. He could keep it warm and pleasant, as his race thought of warmth and pleasantness. Did you notice the light, the color of it?"

McReady nodded. "Beyond the stars is the answer. From beyond the stars. From a hotter planet that circled a brighter, bluer sun they came."

McReady glanced out the door toward the blasted, smoke-stained trail that flopped and wandered blindly off across the drift. "There won't be any more coming. I guess. Sheer accident it landed here, and that was twenty million years ago. What did it do all that for?" He nodded toward the apparatus.

Barclay laughed softly. "Did you notice what it was working on when we came? Look." He pointed toward the ceiling of the shack.

Like a knapsack made of flattened coffee tins, with dangling cloth straps and leather belts, the mechanism clung to the ceiling. A tiny, glaring heart of supernal flame burned

in it, yet burned through the ceiling's wood
without scorching it. Barclay walked over to it,
grasped two of the dangling straps in his
hands, and pulled it down with an effort. He
strapped it about his body. A slight jump
carried him in a weirdly slow arc across the
room.

"Antigravity," said McReady softly.

"Antigravity," Norris nodded. "Yes, we had
'em stopped, with no planes, and no birds. The
birds hadn't come — but it had coffee tins and
radio parts, and glass and the machine shop
at night. And a week — a whole week — all
to itself. America in a single jump — with antigravity powered by the atomic energy of
matter.

"We had 'em stopped. Another half hour —
it was just tightening these straps on the
device so it could wear it — and we'd have
stayed in Antarctica, and shot down any
moving thing that came from the rest of the
world."

"The albatross — " McReady said softly.
"Do you suppose — "

"With this thing almost finished? With that
death weapon it held in its hand?

"No, by the grace of God, who evidently
does hear very well, even down here, and the
margin of half an hour, we keep our world,
and the planets of the system, too. Antigravity, you know, and atomic power. Because They came from another sun, a star
beyond the stars. *They* came from a world with
a bluer sun."

Collecting Team

ROBERT SILVERBERG

When they landed on this planet, they
wore their experience like a badge.
They were Earthmen, kings of the Universe, collectors of exotic life-forms
from the far corners of the galaxy. But
there was something very peculiar
about this planet, especially after *something* or *someone* started sabotaging
their ship. Were those intelligent-
looking zebralike things, just beyond
the port, trying to tell them something?

From fifty thousand miles up, the situation
looked promising. It was a middle-sized,
brown and green, inviting-looking planet, with
no sign of cities or any other such complica-
tions. Just a pleasant sort of place, the very
sort we were looking for to redeem what had
been a pretty futile expedition.

I turned to Clyde Holdreth, who was staring reflectively at the thermocouple.

"Well? What do you think?"

"Looks fine to me. Temperature's about seventy down there — nice and warm, and plenty of air. I think it's worth a try."

Lee Davison came strolling out from the storage hold, smelling of animals, as usual. He was holding one of the blue monkeys we picked up on Alpheraz, and the little beast was crawling up his arm. "Have we found something, gentlemen?"

"We've found a planet," I said. "How's the storage space in the hold?"

"Don't worry about that. We've got room for a whole zooful more before we get filled up. It hasn't been a very fruitful trip."

"No," I agreed. "It hasn't. Well? Shall we go down and see what's to be seen?"

"Might as well," Holdreth said. "We can't go back to Earth with just a couple of blue monkeys and some anteaters, you know."

"I'm in favor of a landing too," said Davison. "You?"

I nodded. "I'll set up the charts, and you get your animals confortable for deceleration."

Davison disappeared back into the storage hold, while Holdreth scribbled furiously in the logbook, writing down the co-ordinates of the planet below, its general description, and so forth. Aside from being a collecting team for the zoological department of the Bureau of Interstellar Affairs, we also double as a survey ship, and the planet down below was listed as *unexplored* on our charts.

I glanced out at the mottled brown and green ball spinning slowly in the viewport, and felt the warning twinge of gloom that came to me every time we made a landing on a new and strange world. Repressing it, I started to figure out a landing orbit. From behind me came the furious chatter of the blue monkeys as Davison strapped them into their acceleration cradles, and under that the deep, unmusical honking of the Rigelian anteaters, noisily bleating their displeasure.

The planet was inhabited, all right. We hadn't had the ship on the ground more than a minute before the local fauna began to congregate. We stood at the viewport and looked out in wonder.

"This is one of those things you dream about," Davison said, stroking his little beard nervously. "Look at them! There must be a thousand different species out there."

"I've never seen anything like it," said Holdreth.

I computed how much storage space we had left and how many of the thronging creatures outside we would be able to bring back with us. "How are we going to decide what to take and what to leave behind?"

"Does it matter?" Holdreth said gaily. "This is what you call an embarrassment of riches, I guess. We just grab the dozen most bizarre creatures and blast off — and save the rest for another trip. It's too bad we wasted all that time wandering around near Rigel."

"We *did* get the anteaters," Davison pointed out. They were his finds, and he was proud of them.

I smiled sourly. "Yeah. We got the anteaters there." The anteaters honked at that moment, loud and clear. "You know, that's one set of beasts I think I could do without."

"Bad attitude," Holdreth said. "Unprofessional."

"Whoever said I was a zoologist, anyway? I'm just a spaceship pilot, remember. And if I don't like the way those anteaters talk — and smell — I see no reason why I — "

"Say, look at that one," Davison said suddenly.

I glanced out the viewport and saw a new beast emerging from the thick-packed vegetation in the background. I've seen some fairly strange creatures since I was assigned to the zoological department, but this one took the grand prize.

It was about the size of a giraffe, moving on long, wobbly legs and with a tiny head up at the end of a preposterous neck. Only it had six legs and a bunch of writhing snakelike tentacles as well, and its eyes, great violet globes, stood out nakedly on the ends of two thick stalks. It must have been twenty feet high. It moved with exaggerated grace through the swarm of beasts surrounding our ship, pushed its way smoothly toward the vessel, and peered gravely in at the viewport. One purple eye stared directly at me, the other at Davison. Oddly, it seemed to me as if it were trying to tell us something.

"Big one, isn't it?" Davison said finally.

"I'll bet you'd like to bring one back, too."

"Maybe we can fit a young one aboard," Davison said. "If we can find a young one." He turned to Holdreth. "How's that air analysis coming? I'd like to get out there and start collecting. God, that's a crazy-looking beast!"

The animal outside had apparently finished its inspection of us, for it pulled its head away and, gathering its legs under itself, squatted near the ship. A small doglike creature with stiff spines running along its back began to bark at the big creature, which took no notice. The other animals, which came in all shapes and sizes, continued to mill around the ship, evidently very curious about the newcomer to their world. I could see Davison's eyes thirsty with the desire to take the whole kit and caboodle back to Earth with him. I knew what was running through his mind. He was dreaming of the umpteen thousand species of extraterrestrial wildlife roaming around out there, and to each one he was attaching a neat little tag: *Something-or-other davisoni.*

"The air's fine," Holdreth announced abruptly, looking up from his test-tubes. "Get your butterfly nets and let's see what we can catch."

There was something I didn't like about the place. It was just too good to be true, and I learned long ago that nothing ever is. There's always a catch someplace.

Only this seemed to be on the level. The planet was a bonanza for zoologists, and Davison and Holdreth were having the time of their lives, hip-deep in obliging specimens.

"I've never seen anything like it," Davison said for at least the fiftieth time, as he scooped up a small purplish squirrel-like creature and examined it curiously. The squirrel stared back, examining Davison just as curiously.

"Let's take some of these," Davison said. "I like them."

"Carry 'em on in, then," I said, shrugging. I didn't care which specimens they chose, so long as they filled up the storage hold quickly and let me blast off on schedule. I watched as Davison grabbed a pair of the squirrels and brought them into the ship.

Holdreth came over to me. He was carrying a sort of dog with insect-faceted eyes and gleaming, furless skin. "How's this one, Gus?"

"Fine," I said bleakly. "Wonderful."

He put the animal down — it didn't scamper away, just sat there smiling at us — and looked at me. He ran a hand through his fast-vanishing hair. "Listen, Gus, you've been gloomy all day. What's eating you?"

"I don't like this place," I said.

"Why? Just on general principles?"

"It's too *easy*, Clyde. Much too easy. These animals just flock around here waiting to be picked up."

Holdreth chuckled. "And you're used to a struggle, aren't you? You're just angry at us because we have it so simple here!"

"When I think of the trouble we went through just to get a pair of miserable vile-smelling anteaters, and — "

"Come off it, Gus. We'll load up in a hurry, if you like. But this place is a zoological gold mine!"

I shook my head. "I don't like it, Clyde. Not at all."

Holdreth laughed again and picked up his faceted-eyed dog. "Say, know where I can find another of these, Gus?"

"Right over there," I said, pointing. "By that tree. With its tongue hanging out. It's just waiting to be carried away."

Holdreth looked and smiled. "What do you know about that!" He snared his specimen and carried both of them inside.

I walked away to survey the grounds. The planet was too flatly incredible for me to accept on face value, without at least a look-see, despite the blithe way my two companions were snapping up specimens.

For one thing, animals just don't exist this way — in big miscellaneous quantities, living all together happily. I hadn't noticed more than a few of each kind, and there must have been five hundred different species, each one stranger-looking than the next. Nature doesn't work that way.

For another, they all seemed to be on friendly terms with one another, though they

acknowledged the unofficial leadership of the
giraffe-like creature. Nature doesn't work *that*
way, either. I hadn't seen one quarrel between the animals yet. That argued that they
were all herbivores, which didn't make sense
ecologically.

I shrugged my shoulders and walked on.

Half an hour later, I knew a little more about
the geography of our bonanza. We were on
either an immense island or a peninsula of
some sort, because I could see a huge body
of water bordering the land some ten miles
off. Our vicinity was fairly flat, except for a
good-sized hill from which I could see the
terrain.

There was a thick, heavily wooded jungle
not too far from the ship. The forest spread
out all the way toward the water in one direction, but ended abruptly in the other. We had
brought the ship down right at the edge of
the clearing. Apparently most of the animals
we saw lived in the jungle.

On the other side of our clearing was a low,
broad plain that seemed to trail away into a
desert in the distance; I could see an un-
inviting stretch of barren sand that contrasted
strangely with the fertile jungle to my left.
There was a small lake to the side. It was, I
saw, the sort of country likely to attract a
varied fauna, since there seemed to be every
sort of habitat within a small area.

And the fauna! Although I'm a zoologist only

by osmosis, picking up both my interest and my knowledge second-hand from Holdreth and Davison, I couldn't help but be astonished by the wealth of strange animals. They came in all different shapes and sizes, colors and odors, and the only thing they all had in common was their friendliness. During the course of my afternoon's wanderings a hundred animals must have come marching boldly right up to me, given me the once-over, and walked away. This included half a dozen kinds that I hadn't seen before, plus one of the eye-stalked, intelligent-looking giraffes and a furless dog. Again, I had the feeling that the giraffe seemed to be trying to communicate.

I didn't like it. I didn't like it at all.

I returned to our clearing, and saw Holdreth and Davison still buzzing madly around, trying to cram as many animals as they could into our hold.

"How's it going?" I asked.

"Hold's all full," Davison said. "We're busy making our alternate selections now." I saw him carrying out Holdreth's two furless dogs and picking up instead a pair of eight-legged penguinish things that uncomplainingly allowed themselves to be carried in. Holdreth was frowning unhappily.

"What do you want *those* for, Lee. Those doglike ones seem much more interesting, don't you think?"

"No," Davison said. "I'd rather bring along

these two. They're curious beasts, aren't they? Look at the muscular network that connects the — "

"Hold it, fellows," I said. I peered at the animal in Davison's hands and glanced up. "This *is* a curious beast," I said. "It's got eight legs."

"You becoming a zoologist?" Holdreth asked, amused.

"No — but I am getting puzzled. Why should this one have eight legs, some of the others here six, and some of the others only four?"

They looked at me blankly, with the scorn of professionals.

"I mean, there ought to be some sort of logic to evolution here, shouldn't there? On Earth we've developed a four-legged pattern of animal life; on Venus, they usually run to six legs. But have you ever seen an evolutionary hodgepodge like this place before?"

"There are stranger setups," Holdreth said. "The symbiotes on Sirius Three, the burrowers of Mizar — but you're right, Gus. This *is* a peculiar evolutionary dispersal. I think we ought to stay and investigate it fully."

Instantly I knew from the bright expression on Davison's face that I had blundered, had made things worse than ever. I decided to take a new tack.

"I don't agree," I said. "I think we ought to leave with what we've got, and come back with a larger expedition later."

Davison chuckled. "Come on, Gus, don't be silly! This is a chance of a lifetime for us —

why should we call in the whole zoological department on it?"

I didn't want to tell them I was afraid of staying longer. I crossed my arms. "Lee, I'm the pilot of this ship, and you'll have to listen to me. The schedule calls for a brief stopover here, and we have to leave. Don't tell me I'm being silly."

"But you are, man! You're standing blindly in the path of scientific investigation, of — "

"Listen to me, Lee. Our food is calculated on a pretty narrow margin, to allow you fellows more room for storage. And this is strictly a collecting team. There's no provision for extended stays on any one planet. Unless you want to wind up eating your own specimens, I suggest you allow us to get out of here."

They were silent for a moment. Then Holdreth said, "I guess we can't argue with that, Lee. Let's listen to Gus and go back now. There's plenty of time to investigate this place later, when we can take longer."

"But — oh, all right," Davison said reluctantly. He picked up the eight-legged penguins. "Let me stash these things in the hold, and we can leave." He looked strangely at me, as if I had done something criminal.

As he started into the ship, I called to him.

"What is it, Gus?"

"Look here, Lee. I don't *want* to pull you away from here. It's simply a matter of food," I lied, masking my nebulous suspicions.

"I know how it is, Gus." He turned and entered the ship.

I stood there thinking about nothing at all for a moment, then went inside myself to begin setting up the blastoff orbit.

I got as far as calculating the fuel expenditure when I noticed something. Feedwires were dangling crazily down from the control cabinet. Somebody had wrecked our drive mechanism, but thoroughly.

For a long moment, I stared stiffly at the sabotaged drive. Then I turned and headed into the storage hold.

"Davison?"

"What is it, Gus?"

"Come out here a second, will you?"

I waited, and a few minutes later he appeared, frowning impatiently. "What do you want. Gus? I'm busy and I — " His mouth dropped open. "*Look at the drive!*"

"You look at it," I snapped. "I'm sick. Go get Holdreth, on the double."

While he was gone I tinkered with the shattered mechanism. Once I had the cabinet panel off and could see the inside, I felt a little better; the drive wasn't damaged beyond repair, though it had been pretty well scrambled. Three or four days of hard work with a screwdriver and solderbeam might get the ship back into functioning order.

But that didn't make me any less angry. I heard Holdreth and Davison entering behind me, and I whirled to face them.

"All right, you idiots. Which one of you did this?"

They opened their mouths in protesting

squawks at the same instant. I listened to them for a while, then said, "One at a time!"

"If you're implying that one of us deliberately sabotaged the ship," Holdreth said, "I want you to know — "

"I'm not implying anything. But the way it looks to me, you two decided you'd like to stay here a while longer to continue your investigations, and figured the easiest way of getting me to agree was to wreck the drive." I glared hotly at them. "Well, I've got news for you. I can fix this, and I can fix it in a couple of days. So go on — get about your business! Get all the zoologizing you can in, while you still have time. I — "

Davison laid a hand gently on my arm. "Gus," he said quietly, *"We didn't do it. Neither of us."*

Suddenly all the anger drained out of me and was replaced by raw fear. I could see that Davison meant it.

"If you didn't do it, and Holdreth didn't do it, and *I* didn't do it — then who did?"

Davison shrugged.

"Maybe it's one of us who doesn't know he's doing it," I suggested. "Maybe — " I stopped. "Oh, that's nonsense. Hand me that tool-kit, will you, Lee?"

They left to tend to the animals, and I set to work on the repair job, dismissing all further speculations and suspicions from my mind, concentrating solely on joining Lead A to Input A and Transistor F to Potentiometer K, as indicated. It was slow, nerve-harrowing

work, and by mealtime I had accomplished
only the barest preliminaries. My fingers were
starting to quiver from the strain of small-
scale work, and I decided to give up the job
for the day and get back to it tomorrow.

I slept uneasily, my nightmares punctuated
by the moaning of the accursed anteaters and
the occasional squeals, chuckles, bleats, and
hisses of the various other creatures in the
hold. It must have been four in the morning
before I dropped off into a really sound sleep,
and what was left of the night passed swiftly.
The next thing I knew, hands were shaking
me, and I was looking up into the pale, tense
faces of Holdreth and Davison.

I pushed my sleep-stuck eyes open and
blinked. "Huh? What's going on?"

Holdreth leaned down and shook me
savagely. "Get up, Gus!"

I struggled to my feet slowly. "Hell of a
thing to do, wake a fellow up in the middle
of the — "

I found myself being propelled from my
cabin and led down the corridor to the control
room. Blearily, I followed where Holdreth
pointed, and then I woke up in a hurry.

The drive was battered again. Someone —
or *something* — had completely undone my
repair job of the night before.

If there had been bickering among us, it
stopped. This was past the category of a joke
now; it couldn't be laughed off, and we found
ourselves working together as a tight unit

again, trying desperately to solve the puzzle before it was too late.

"Let's review the situation," Holdreth said, pacing nervously up and down the control cabin. "The drive has been sabotaged twice. None of us knows who did it, and on a conscious level each of us is convinced *he* didn't do it."

He paused. "That leaves us with two possibilities. Either, as Gus suggested, one of us is doing it unaware of it even himself, or someone else is doing it while we're not looking. Neither possibility is a very cheerful one."

"We can stay on guard, though," I said. "Here's what I propose: first, have one of us awake at all times — sleep in shifts, that is, with somebody guarding the drive until I get it fixed. Two — jettison all the animals aboard ship."

"What?"

"He's right," Davison said. "We don't know what we may have brought aboard. They don't seem to be intelligent, but we can't be sure. That purple-eyed baby giraffe, for instance — suppose he's been hypnotizing us into damaging the drive ourselves? How can we tell?"

"Oh, but — " Holdreth started to protest, then stopped and frowned soberly. "I suppose we'll have to admit the possibility," he said, obviously unhappy about the prospect of freeing our captives. "We'll empty out the hold, and you see if you can get the drive fixed.

Maybe later we'll recapture them all, if nothing further develops."

We agreed to that, and Holdreth and Davison cleared the ship of its animal cargo while I set to work determinedly at the drive mechanism. By nightfall, I had managed to accomplish as much as I had the day before.

I sat up as watch the first shift, aboard the strangely quiet ship. I paced around the cabin, fighting the great temptation to doze off, and managed to last through until the time Holdreth arrived to relieve me.

Only — when he showed up, he gasped and pointed at the drive. It had been ripped apart a third time.

Now we had no excuse, no explanation. The expedition had turned into a nightmare.

I could only protest that I had remained awake my entire spell on duty, and that I had seen no one and no thing approach the drive panel. But that was hardly a satisfactory explanation, since it either cast guilt on me as the saboteur or implied that some unseen external power was repeatedly wrecking the drive. Neither hypothesis made sense, at least to me.

By now we had spent four days on the planet, and food was getting to be a major problem. My carefully budgeted flight schedule called for us to be two days out on our return to Earth by now. But we still were no closer to departure than we had been four days ago.

The animals continued to wander around outside, nosing up against the ship, examining it, almost fondling it, with those damned pseudo-giraffes staring soulfully at us always. The beasts were as friendly as ever, little knowing how the tension was growing within the hull. The three of us walked around like zombies, eyes bright and lips clamped. We were scared — all of us.

Something was keeping us from fixing the drive.

Something didn't want us to leave this planet.

I looked at the bland face of the purple-eyed giraffe staring through the viewport, and it stared mildly back at me. Around it was grouped the rest of the local fauna, the same incredible hodgepodge of improbable genera and species.

That night, the three of us stood guard in the control-room together. The drive was smashed anyway. The wires were soldered in so many places by now that the control panel was a mass of shining alloy, and I knew that a few more such sabotagings and it would be impossible to patch it together any more — if it wasn't so already.

The next night, I just didn't knock off. I continued soldering right on after dinner (and a pretty skimpy dinner it was, now that we were on close rations) and far on into the night.

By morning, it was as if I hadn't done a thing.

"I give up," I announced, surveying the damage. "I don't see any sense in ruining my nerves trying to fix a thing that won't stay fixed."

Holdreth nodded. He looked terribly pale. "We'll have to find some new approach."

I yanked open the food closet and examined our stock. Even figuring in the synthetics we would have fed to the animals if we hadn't released them, we were low on food. We had overstayed even the safety margin. It would be a hungry trip back — if we ever did get back.

I clambered through the hatch and sprawled down on a big rock near the ship. One of the furless dogs came over and muzzled in my shirt. Davison stepped to the hatch and called down to me.

"What are you doing out there, Gus?"

"Just getting a little fresh air. I'm sick of living aboard that ship." I scratched the dog behind his pointed ears, and looked around.

The animals had lost most of their curiosity about us, and didn't congregate the way they used to. They were meandering all over the plain, nibbling at little deposits of a white doughy substance. It precipitated every night. "Manna," we called it. All the animals seemed to live on it.

I folded my arms and leaned back.

We were getting to look awfully lean by the eighth day. I wasn't even trying to fix the ship any more; the hunger was starting to get me.

But I saw Davison puttering around with my solderbeam.

"What are you doing?"

"I'm going to repair the drive," he said. "You don't want to, but we can't just sit around, you know." His nose was deep in my repair guide, and he was fumbling with the release on the solderbeam.

I shrugged. "Go ahead, if you want to." I didn't care what he did. All I cared about was the gaping emptiness in my stomach, and about the dimly grasped fact that somehow we were stuck here for good.

"Gus?"

"Yeah?"

"I think it's time I told you something. I've been eating the manna for four days. It's good. It's nourishing stuff."

"You've been eating — the manna? Something that grows on an alien world? You crazy?"

"What else can we do? Starve?"

I smiled feebly, admitting that he was right. From somewhere in the back of the ship came the sounds of Holdreth moving around. Holdreth had taken this thing worse than any of us. He had a family back on Earth, and he was beginning to realize that he wasn't ever going to see them again.

"Why don't you get Holdreth?" Davison suggested. "Go out there and stuff yourselves with the manna. You've got to eat something."

"Yeah. What can I lose?" Moving like a mechanical man, I headed toward Holdreth's cabin. We would go out and eat the manna and cease being hungry, one way or another.

"Clyde?" I called. "Clyde?"

I entered his cabin. He was sitting at his desk, shaking convulsively, staring at the two streams of blood that trickled in red spurts from his slashed wrists.

"Clyde!"

He made no protest as I dragged him toward the infirmary cabin and got tourniquets around his arms, cutting off the bleeding. He just stared dully ahead, sobbing.

I slapped him and he came around. He shook his head dizzily, as if he didn't know where he was.

"I — I — "

"Easy, Clyde. Everything's all right."

"It's *not* all right," he said hollowly. "I'm still alive. Why didn't you let me die? Why didn't you — "

Davison entered the cabin. "What's been happening, Gus?"

"It's Clyde. The pressure's getting him. He tried to kill himself, but I think he's all right now. Get him something to eat, will you?"

We had Holdreth straightened around by evening. Davison gathered as much of the manna as he could find, and we held a feast.

"I wish we had nerve enough to kill some of the local fauna," Davison said. "Then we'd have a feast — steaks and everything!"

"The bacteria," Holdreth pointed out quietly. "We don't dare."

"I know. But it's a thought."

"No more thoughts," I said sharply. "To-morrow morning we start work on the drive panel again. Maybe with some food in our bellies we'll be able to keep awake and see what's happening here."

Holdreth smiled. "Good. I can't wait to get out of this ship and back to a normal existence. God, I just can't wait!"

"Let's get some sleep," I said. "Tomorrow we'll give it another try. We'll get back," I said with a confidence I didn't feel.

The following morning I rose early and got my tool-kit. My head was clear, and I was trying to put the pieces together without much luck. I started toward the control cabin.

And stopped.

And looked out the viewport.

I went back and awoke Holdreth and Davison. "Take a look out the port," I said hoarsely.

They looked. They gaped.

"It looks just like my house," Holdreth said. "My house on Earth."

"With all the comforts of home inside, I'll bet." I walked forward uneasily and lowered myself through the hatch. "Let's go look at it."

We approached it, while the animals frolicked around us. The big giraffe came near and shook its head gravely. The house stood in the middle of the clearing, small and neat and freshly painted.

I saw it now. During the night, invisible hands had put it there, had assembled and

built a cozy little Earth-type house and
dropped it next to our ship for us to live in.

"Just like my house," Holdreth repeated in
wonderment.

"It should be," I said. "They grabbed the
model from your mind, as soon as they found
out we couldn't live on the ship indefinitely."

Holdreth and Davison asked as one, "What
do you mean?"

"You mean you haven't figured this place
out yet?" I licked my lips, getting myself used
to the fact that I was going to spend the rest
of my life here. "You mean you don't realize
what this house is intended to be?"

They shook their heads, baffled. I glanced
around, from the house to the useless ship to
the jungle to the plain to the little pond. It all
made sense now.

"They want to keep us happy," I said. "They
knew we weren't thriving aboard the ship, so
they — they built us something a little more
like home."

"*They?* The giraffes?"

"Forget the giraffes. They tried to warn us,
but it's too late. They're intelligent beings, but
they're prisoners just like us. I'm talking about
the ones who run this place. The super-aliens
who make us sabotage our own ship and not
even know we're doing it, who stand someplace up there and gape at us. The ones who
dredged together this motley assortment of
beasts from all over the galaxy. Now we've
been collected too. This whole damned place
is just a zoo — a zoo for aliens so far ahead

of us we don't dare dream what they're like."

I looked up at the shimmering blue-green sky, where invisible bars seemed to restrain us, and sank down dismally on the porch of our new home. I was resigned. There wasn't any sense in struggling against *them*.

I could see the neat little placard now,

EARTHMEN.
Native Habitat, Sol III.

The Haunted
Space Suit

ARTHUR C. CLARKE

As he launched himself into space, he
knew something was horribly wrong.
Besides the familiar, faint sounds of his
space suit, his keen ears detected some
unusual and disturbing new noises. Was
it the ghost of the suit's previous owner,
restless within its old "skin"? What happens to the soul of a man who dies between the stars, light-years from his
native world?

When Satellite Control called me, I was writing up the day's progress report in the ob-
servation bubble — the glass-domed office
that juts out from the axis of the space
station like the hubcap of a wheel.

It was not really a good place to work, for
the view was too overwhelming. Only a few
yards away I could see the construction teams
performing their slow-motion ballet as they
put the station together like a giant jigsaw

puzzle. And beyond them, twenty thousand miles below, was the blue-green glory of the full Earth, floating against the raveled star-clouds.

"Station supervisor here," I answered. "What's the trouble?"

"Our radar's showing a small echo two miles away, almost stationary, about five degrees west of Sirius. Can you give us a visual report on it?"

Anything matching our orbit so precisely could hardly be a meteor; it would have to be something we'd dropped — perhaps an inadequately secured piece of equipment that had drifted away from the station. So I assumed; but when I pulled out my binoculars and searched the sky around Orion, I soon found my mistake. Though this space traveler was man-made, it had nothing to do with us.

"I've found it," I told Control. "It's someone's test satellite — cone-shaped, four antennas. Probably U.S. Air Force, early 1960's, judging by the design. I know they lost track of several when their transmitters failed. There were quite a few attempts to hit this orbit before they finally made it."

After a brief search through the files, Control was able to confirm my guess. It was a little longer to find that now, in 1988, Washington wasn't in the least bit interested in our discovery and would be just as happy if we lost it again.

"Well, we can't do *that*," said Control.

"Even if nobody wants it, the thing's a menace to navigation. Someone had better go out and haul it aboard; get it out of orbit."

That someone, I realized, would have to be me. I dared not detach a man from the closely knit construction teams; we were already behind schedule, and a single day's delay on this job cost a million dollars. All the radio and TV networks on Earth were waiting impatiently for the moment when they could route their programs through us, and thus provide the first truly global service, spanning the world from pole to pole.

"I'll go out and get it," I answered, and though I tried to sound as if I were doing everyone a great favor, I was secretly not at all displeased. It had been at least two weeks since I'd been outside.

The only member of the staff I passed on my way to the air lock was Tommy, our recently acquired cat. Pets mean a great deal to men thousands of miles from Earth, but there are not many animals that can adapt themselves to a weightless environment. Tommy mewed plaintively at me as I clambered into my spacesuit, but I was in too much of a hurry to play with him.

At this point, perhaps I should remind you that the suits we use on the station are completely different from the flexible affairs men wear when they want to walk around on the Moon. Ours are really baby space ships, just big enough to hold one man. They are stubby cylinders, about seven feet long, fitted with low-powered propulsion jets, and have a pair of accordionlike sleeves at the upper end for the operator's arms.

As soon as I'd settled down inside my very exclusive space craft, I switched on power and checked the gauges on the tiny instrument panel. All my needles were well in the safety zone, so I gave Tommy a wink for luck, lowered the transparent hemisphere over my head, and sealed myself in. For a short trip like this, I did not bother to check the suit's internal lockers, which were used to carry food and special equipment for extended missions.

As the conveyor belt decanted me into the air lock, I felt like an Indian papoose being carried along on its mother's back. Then the pumps brought the pressure down to zero, the outer door opened, and the last traces of air swept me out into the stars, turning very slowly head over heels.

The station was only a dozen feet away, yet I was now an independent planet — a little world of my own. I was sealed up in a tiny, mobile cylinder, with a superb view of the entire universe, but I had practically no freedom of movement inside the suit. The padded seat and safety belts prevented me from turning around, though I could reach all the controls and lockers with my hands or feet.

In space, the great enemy is the Sun, which can blast you to blindness in seconds. Very cautiously, I opened up the dark filters on the "night" side of my suit, and turned my head to look out at the stars. At the same time I switched the helmet's external sunshade to automatic, so that whichever way the suit gyrated my eyes would be shielded.

Presently, I found my target — a bright fleck of silver whose metallic glint distinguished it clearly from the surrounding stars. I stamped on the jet control pedal and felt the mild surge of acceleration as the low-powered rockets set me moving away from the station. After ten seconds of steady thrust, I cut off the drive. It would take me five minutes to coast the rest of the way, and not much longer to return with my salvage.

And it was at that moment, as I launched myself out into the abyss, that I knew that something was horribly wrong.

It is never completely silent inside a space suit; you can always hear the gentle hiss of oxygen, the faint whir of fans and motors, the susurration of your own breathing — even, if you listen carefully enough, the rhythmic thump that is the pounding of your heart. These sounds reverberate through the suit, unable to escape into the surrounding void; they are the unnoticed background of life in space, for you are aware of them only when they change.

They had changed now; to them had been added a sound which I could not identify. It was an intermittent, muffled thudding, sometimes accompanied by a scraping noise.

I froze instantly, holding my breath and

trying to locate the alien sound with my ears. The meters on the control board gave no clues; all the needles were rock-steady on their scales, and there were none of the flickering red lights that would warn of impending disaster. That was some comfort, but not much. I had long ago learned to trust my instincts in such matters; it was their alarm signals that were flashing now, telling me to return to the station before it was too late. . . .

Even now, I do not like to recall those next few minutes, as panic slowly flooded into my mind like a rising tide, overwhelming the dikes of reason and logic which every man must erect against the mystery of the universe. I knew then what it was like to face insanity; no other explanation fitted the facts.

For it was no longer possible to pretend that the noise disturbing me was that of some faulty mechanism. Though I was in utter isolation, far from any other human being or indeed any material object, I was not alone. The soundless void was bringing to my ears the faint, but unmistakable, stirrings of life.

In that first, heart-freezing moment it seemed that something was trying to get into my suit — something invisible, seeking shelter from the cruel and pitiless vacuum of space. I whirled madly in my harness, scanning the entire sphere of vision around me except for the blazing, forbidden cone toward the Sun. There was nothing there, of course. There could not be — yet that purposeful scrabbling was clearer than ever.

Despite the nonsense that has been written about is, it is not true that spacemen are superstitious. But can you blame me if, as I came to the end of logic's resources, I suddenly remembered how Bernie Summers had died, no further from the station than I was at this very moment?

It was one of those "impossible" accidents; it always is. Three things had gone wrong at once. Bernie's oxygen regulator had run wild and sent the pressure soaring, the safety valve had failed to blow, and a faulty joint had given way. In a fraction of a second, his suit was open to space.

I had never known Bernie, but suddenly his fate became of overwhelming importance to me, for a horrible idea had come into my mind. One does not talk about these things, but a damaged space suit is too valuable to be thrown away, even if it has killed its wearer. It is repaired, renumbered — and issued to someone else. . . .

What happens to the soul of a man who dies between the stars, far from his native world? Were you still here, Bernie, clinging to the last object that linked you to your lost and distant home?

As I fought the nightmares that were swirling around me — for now it seemed that the scratchings and soft fumblings were coming from all directions — there was one last hope to which I clung. For the sake of sanity, I had to prove that this wasn't Bernie's suit — that the metal walls so closely wrapped around me had never been another man's coffin.

It took me several tries before I could press the right button and switch my transmitter to the emergency wave length. "Station!" I gasped, "I'm in trouble! Get records to check my suit — "

I never finished; they say my yell wrecked the microphone. But what man, alone in the absolute isolation of space, would *not* have yelled when something patted him softly on the back of the neck?

I must have lunged forward, despite the safety harness, and smashed against the upper edge of the control panel. When the rescue squad reached me a few minutes later, I was still unconscious, with an angry bruise across my forehead.

And so I was the last person in the whole satellite relay system to know what had happened. When I came to my senses an hour later, all our medical staff was gathered around my bed, but it was quite a while before the doctors — and certainly that cute little space nurse — bothered to look at me. They were much too busy playing with the three little kittens our badly misnamed Tommy had been rearing in my space suit's Number Three storage locker.

Condition of Employment

CLIFFORD D. SIMAK

Someday he'd find a ship that would take him home . . . home to Mars. What he had here on Earth was more than simple homesickness: It was planetsickness, culturesickness, a cutting off of all he'd ever known or wanted. He'd been a fool for ever going into space. Let him just get back to Mars and no one could ever get him off it. Or so he thought. . . .

He had been dreaming of home, and when he came awake, he held his eyes tight shut in a desperate effort not to lose the dream. He kept some of it, but it was blurred and faint and lacked the sharp distinction and the color of the dream. He could tell it to himself, he knew just how it was, he could recall it as a lost and far-off thing and place, but it was not there as it had been in the dream.

But even so, he held his eyes tight shut, for now that he was awake, he knew what they'd

open on, and he shrank from the drabness and
the coldness of the room in which he lay. It
was, he thought, not alone the drabness and
the cold, but also the loneliness and the sense
of not belonging. So long as he did not look
at it, he need not accept this harsh reality,
although he felt himself on the fringe of it,
and it was reaching for him, reaching through
the color and the warmth and friendliness of
this other place he tried to keep in mind.

At last it was impossible. The fabric of the
held-onto dream became too thin and fragile
to ward off the moment of reality, and he let
his eyes come open.

It was every bit as bad as he remembered
it. It was drab and cold and harsh, and there
was the maddening alienness waiting for him,
crouching in the corner. He tensed himself
against it, trying to work up his courage,
hardening himself to arise and face it for
another day.

The plaster of the ceiling was cracked and
had flaked away in great ugly blotches. The
paint on the wall was peeling and dark stains
ran down it from the times the rain leaked in.
And there was the smell, the musty human
smell that had been caged in the room too
long.

Staring at the ceiling, he tried to see the
sky. There had been a time when he could
have seen it through this or any ceiling. For
the sky had belonged to him, the sky and the
wild, dark space beyond it. But now he'd lost
them. They were his no longer.

A few marks in a book, he thought, an entry in the record. That was all that was needed to smash a man's career, to crush his hope forever, and to keep him wrapped and exiled on a planet that was not his own.

He sat up and swung his feet over the edge of the bed, hunting for the trousers he'd left on the floor. He found and pulled them on and scuffed into his shoes and stood up in the room.

The room was small and mean — and cheap. There would come a day when he could not afford a room even as cheap as this. His cash was running out, and when the last of it was gone, he would have to get some job, any kind of job. Perhaps he should have gotten one before he began to run so short. But he had shied away from it. For settling down to work would be an admission that he was defeated, that he had given up his hope of going home again.

He had been a fool, he told himself, for ever going into space. Let him just get back to Mars and no one could ever get him off it. He'd go back to the ranch and stay there as his father had wanted him to do. He'd marry Ellen and settle down, and other fools could fly the death-traps around the Solar System.

Glamor, he thought — it was the glamor that sucked in the kids when they were young and starry-eyed. The glamor of the far place, of the wilderness of space, of the white eyes of the stars watching in that wilderness — the glamor of the engine-song and of the chill white metal knifing through the blackness, and the loneliness of the emptiness, and the few cubic feet of courage and defiance that thumbed its nose at that emptiness.

But there was no glamor. There was brutal work and everlasting watchfulness and awful sickness, the terrible fear that listened for the stutter in the drive, for the *ping* against the metal hide, for any one of the thousand things that could happen out in space.

He picked up his wallet off the bedside table and put it in his pocket and went out into the hall and down the rickety stairs to the crumbling, lopsided porch outside.

And the greenness waited for him, the unrelenting, bilious green of Earth. It was a thing to gag at, to steel oneself against, an indecent and abhorrent color for anyone to look at. The grass was green and all the plants and every single tree. There was no place outdoors and few indoors where one could escape from it, and when one looked at it too long, it seemed to pulse and tremble with a hidden life.

The greenness, and the brightness of the sun, and the sapping heat — these were things of Earth that it was hard to bear. The light one could get away from, and the heat one could somehow ride along with — but the green was always there.

He went down the steps, fumbling in his pocket for a cigarette. He found a crumpled package and in it one crumpled cigarette. He

put it between his lips and threw the pack
away and stood at the gate, trying to make
up his mind.

But it was a gesture only, this hardening of
his mind, for he knew what he would do.
There was nothing else to do. He'd done it
day after day for more weeks than he cared to
count, and he'd do it again today and tomorrow
and tomorrow, until his cash ran out.

And after that, he wondered, what?

Get a job and try to strike a bargain with his
situation? Try to save against the day when
he could buy passage back to Mars — for
they'd surely let him ride the ships even if
they wouldn't let him run them. But, he told
himself, he'd figured that one out. It would
take twenty years to save enough, and he had
no twenty years.

He lit the cigarette and went tramping down
the street, and even through the cigarette, he
could smell the hated green.

Ten blocks later, he reached the far edge of
the spaceport. There was a ship. He stood for
a moment looking at it before he went into the
shabby restaurant to buy himself some breakfast.

There was a ship, he thought, and that was
a hopeful sign. Some days there weren't any,
some days three or four. But there was a ship
today and it might be the one.

One day, he told himself, he'd surely find
the ship out there that would take him home
— a ship with a captain so desperate for an

engineer that he would overlook the entry in the book.

But even as he thought it, he knew it for a lie — a lie he told himself each day. Perhaps to justify his coming here each day to check at the hiring hall, a lie to keep his hope alive, to keep his courage up. A lie that made it even barely possible to face the bleak, warm room and the green of Earth.

He went into the restaurant and sat down on a stool.

The waitress came to take his order. "Cakes again?" she asked.

He nodded. Pancakes were cheap and filling, and he had to make his money last.

"You'll find a ship today," said the waitress. "I have a feeling you will."

"Perhaps I will," he said, without believing it.

"I know just how you feel," the waitress told him. "I know how awful it can be. I was homesick once myself, the first time I left home. I thought I would die."

He didn't answer, for he felt it would not have been dignified to answer. Although why he should now lay claim to dignity, he could not imagine.

But this, in any case, was more than simple homesickness. It was planetsickness, culture-sickness, a cutting off of all he'd known and wanted.

Sitting, waiting for the cakes to cook, he caught the dream again — the dream of red hills rolling far into the land, of the cold, dry air soft against the skin, of the splendor of the stars at twilight, and the fairy yellow of the distant sandstorm. And the low house crouched against the land, with the old gray-haired man sitting stiffly in a chair upon the porch that faced toward the sunset.

The waitress brought the cakes.

The day would come, he told himself, when he could afford no longer this self-pity he carried. He knew it for what it was and he should get rid of it. And yet it was a thing he lived with — even more than that, it had become a way of life. It was his comfort and his shield, the driving force that kept him trudging on each day.

He finished the cakes and paid for them.

"Good luck," said the waitress, with a smile.

"Thank you," he said.

He tramped down the road, with the gravel crunching underfoot and the sun like a blast upon his back, but he had left the greenness. The port lay bare and bald, scalped and cauterized.

He reached where he was going and went up to the desk.

"You again," said the union agent.

"Anything for Mars?"

"Not a thing. No, wait a minute. There was a man in here not too long ago."

The agent got up from the desk and went to the door. Then he stepped outside the door and began to shout at someone.

A few minutes later, he was back. Behind

him came a lumbering and irate individual. He had a cap upon his head that said CAPTAIN in greasy, torn letters, but aside from that he was distinctly out of uniform.

"Here's the man," the agent told the captain. "Name of Anson Cooper. Engineer first class, but his record's not too good."

"Damn the record!" bawled the captain. He said to Cooper: "Do you know Morrisons?"

"I was raised with them," said Cooper. It was not the truth, but he knew he could get by.

"They're good engines," said the captain, "but cranky and demanding. You'll have to baby them. You'll have to sleep with them. And if you don't watch them close, they'll up and break your back."

"I know how to handle them," said Cooper.

"My engineer ran out on me." The captain spat on the floor to show his contempt for runaway engineers. "He wasn't man enough."

"I'm man enough," Cooper declared.

And he knew, standing there, what it would be like. But there was no other choice. If he wanted to get back to Mars, he had to take the Morrisons.

"OK then, come on with you," the captain said.

"Wait a minute," said the union agent. "You can't rush off a man like this. You have to give him time to pick up his duffle."

"I haven't any to pick up," Cooper said, thinking of the few pitiful belongings back in the boarding house. "Or none that matters."

"You understand," the agent said to the captain, "that the union cannot vouch for a man with a record such as his."

"To hell with that," said the captain. "Just so he can run the engines. That's all I ask."

The ship stood far out in the field. She had not been much to start with and she had not improved with age. Just the job of riding on a craft like that would be high torture, without the worry of nursing Morrisons.

"She'll hang together, no fear," said the captain. "She's got a lot more trips left in her than you'd think. It beats all hell what a tub like that can take."

Just one more trip, thought Cooper. Just so she gets me to Mars. Then she can fall apart, for all I care.

"She's beautiful," he said, and meant it.

He walked up to one of the great landing fins and laid a hand upon it. It was solid metal, with all the paint peeled off it, with tiny pits of corrosion speckling its surface, and with a hint of cold, as if it might not as yet have shed all the touch of space.

And this was it, he thought. After all the weeks of waiting, here finally was the thing of steel and engineering that would take him home again.

He walked back to where the captain stood.

"Let's get on with it," he said. "I'll want to look the engines over."

"They're all right," said the captain.

"That may be so. I still want to run a check on them."

He had expected the engines to be bad, but not as bad as they turned out to be. If the ship had not been much to look at, the Morrisons were worse.

"They'll need some work," he said. "We can't lift with them, the shape they're in."

The captain raved and swore. "We have to blast by dawn, damn it! This is a goddam emergency."

"You'll lift by dawn," snapped Cooper. "Just leave me alone."

He drove his gang to work, and he worked himself, for fourteen solid hours, without a wink of sleep, without a bite to eat.

Then he crossed his fingers and told the captain he was ready.

They got out of atmosphere with the engines holding together. Cooper uncrossed the fingers and sighed with deep relief. Now all he had to do was keep them running.

The captain called him forward and brought out a bottle. "You did better, Mr. Cooper, than I thought you would."

Cooper shook his head. "We aren't there yet, Captain. We've a long way still to go."

"Mr. Cooper," said the captain, "you know what we are carrying? You got any idea at all?"

Cooper shook his head.

"Medicines," the captain told him. "There's an epidemic out there. We were the only ship anywhere near ready for takeoff. So we were requisitioned."

"It would have been much better if we could have overhauled the engines."

"We didn't have the time. Every minute counts."

Cooper drank the liquor, stupid with a tiredness that cut clear to the bone. "Epidemic, you say. What kind?"

"Sand fever," said the captain. "You've heard of it, perhaps."

Cooper felt the chill of deadly fear creep along his body. "I've heard of it." He finished off the whisky and stood up. "I have to get back, sir. I have to watch those engines."

"We're counting on you, Mr. Cooper. You have to get us through."

He went back to the engine room and slumped into a chair, listening to the engine-song that beat throughout the ship.

He had to keep them going. There was no question of it now, if there'd even been a question. For now it was not the simple matter of getting home again, but of getting needed drugs to the old home planet.

"I promise you," he said, talking to himself. "I promise you we'll get there."

He drove the engine crew and he drove himself, day after dying day, while the howling of the tubes and the thunder of the haywire Morrisons racked a man almost beyond endurance.

There was no such thing as sleep — only catnaps caught as one could catch them. There were no such things as meals, only food gulped on the run. And there was work, and worse than work were the watching and the waiting, the shoulders tensed against the stutter, or the sudden screech of metal that would spell disaster.

Why, he wondered dully, did a man ever go to space? Why should one deliberately choose a job like this? Here in the engine room, with its cranky motors, it might be worse than elsewhere in the ship. But that didn't mean it wasn't bad. For throughout the ship stretched tension and discomfort and, above all, the dead, black fear of space itself, of what space could do to a ship and the men within it.

In some of the bigger, newer ships, conditions might be better, but not a great deal better. They still tranquilized the passengers and colonists who went out to the other planets — tranquilized them to quiet the worries, to make them more insensitive to discomfort, to prevent their breaking into panic.

But a crew you could not tranquilize. A crew must be wide-awake, with all its faculties intact. A crew had to sit and take it.

Perhaps the time would come when the ships were big enough, when the engines and the drives would be perfected, when Man had lost some of his fear of the emptiness of space — then it would be easier.

But the time might be far off. It was almost two hundred years now since his family had gone out, among the first colonists, to Mars.

If it were not that he was going home, he told himself, it would be beyond all tolerance and endurance. He could almost smell the cold, dry air of home — even in this place that reeked with other smells. He could look beyond the metal skin of the ship in which he rode and across the long dark miles and see the gentle sunset on the redness of the hills.

And in this he had an advantage over all the others. For without going home, he could not have stood it.

The days wore on and the engines held and the hope built up within him. And finally hope gave way to triumph.

And then came the day when the ship went mushing down through the thin, cold atmosphere, and came in to a landing.

He reached out and pulled a switch and the engines rumbled to a halt. Silence came into the tortured steel that still was numb with noise.

He stood beside the engines, deafened by the silence, frightened by this alien thing that never made a sound.

He walked along the engines, with his hand sliding on their metal, stroking them as he would pet an animal, astonished and slightly angry at himself for finding in himself a queer, distorted quality of affection for them.

But why not? They had brought him home. He had nursed and pampered them, he had cursed them and watched over them, he had slept with them, and they had brought him home.

And that was more, he admitted to himself, then he had ever thought they would do.

He found that he was alone. The crew had gone swarming up the ladder as soon as he had pulled the switch. And now it was time that he himself was going.

But he stood there for a moment, in that silent room, as he gave the place one final visual check. Everything was all right. There was nothing to be done.

He turned and climbed the ladder slowly, heading for the port.

He found the captain standing in the port, and out beyond the port stretched the redness of the land.

"All the rest have gone except the purser," said the captain. "I thought you'd soon be up. You did a fine job with the engines, Mr. Cooper. I'm glad you shipped with us."

"It's my last run," Cooper said, staring out at the redness of the hills. "Now I settle down."

"That's strange," said the captain. "I take it you're a Mars man."

"I am. And I never should have left."

The captain stared at him and said again: "That's strange."

"Nothing strange," said Cooper. "I — "

"It's my last run, too," the captain broke in. "There'll be a new commander to take her back to Earth."

"In that case," Cooper offered, "I'll stand you a drink as soon as we get down."

"I'll take you up on that. First we'll get our shots."

They climbed down the ladder and walked across the field toward the spaceport buildings. Trucks went whining past them, heading for the ship, to pick up the unloaded cargo.

And now it was all coming back to Cooper, the way he had dreamed it in that shabby room on Earth — the exhilarating taste of the thinner, colder air, the step that was springier because of the lesser gravity, the swift and clean elation of the uncluttered, brave red land beneath a weaker sun.

Inside, the doctor waited for them in his tiny office.

"Sorry, gentlemen," he said, "but you know the regulations."

"I don't like it," said the captain, "but I suppose it does make sense."

They sat down in the chairs and rolled up their sleeves.

"Hang on," the doctor told them. "It gives you quite a jolt."

It did.

And it had before, thought Cooper, every time before. He should be used to it by now.

He sat weakly in the chair, waiting for the weakness and the shock to pass, and he saw the doctor, there behind his desk, watching them and waiting for them to come around to normal.

"Was it a rough trip?" the doctor finally asked.

"They are all rough," the captain replied curtly.

Cooper shook his head. "This one was the worst I've ever known. Those engines . . ."

The captain said: "I'm sorry, Cooper. This time it was the truth. We were *really* carrying medicine. There *is* an epidemic. Mine was the only ship. I'd planned an overhaul, but we couldn't wait."

Cooper nodded. "I remember now," he said.

He stood up weakly and stared out the window at the cold, the alien, the forbidding land of Mars.

"I never could have made it," he said flatly, "if I'd not been psyched."

He turned back to the doctor. "Will there ever be a time?"

The doctor nodded. "Some day, certainly. When the ships are better. When the race is more conditioned to space travel."

"But this homesickness business — it gets downright brutal."

"It's the only way," the doctor declared. "We'd not have any spacemen if they weren't always going home."

"That's right," the captain said. "No man, myself included, could face that kind of beating unless it was for something more than money."

Cooper looked out the window at the

Martian sandscape and shivered. Of all the God-forsaken places he had ever seen!

He was a fool to be in space, he told himself, with a wife like Doris and two kids back home. He could hardly wait to see them.

And he knew the symptoms. He was getting homesick once again — but this time it was for Earth.

The doctor was taking a bottle out of his desk and pouring generous drinks into glasses for all three of them.

"Have a shot of this," he said, "and let's forget about it."

"As if we could remember," said Cooper, laughing suddenly.

"After all," the captain said, far too cheerfully, "we have to see it in the right perspective. It's nothing more than a condition of employment."

After
the Sirens

HUGH HOOD

"This is not an exercise. This is not an exercise. This is not an exercise," the radio blared. "This is an air raid warning. We will be attacked in fifteen minutes. We will be attacked in fifteen minutes. This is not an exercise." The voice paused, then went on: "Correction. Correction. You have fourteen minutes. In fourteen minutes we will be attacked."

They heard the sirens first about four forty-five in the morning. It was still dark and cold outside and they were sound asleep. They heard the noise first in their dreams and, waking, understood it to be real.

"What is it?" she asked him sleepily, rolling over in their warm bed. "Is there a fire?"

"I don't know," he said. "I've never heard anything like that before."

"It's some kind of siren," she said, "downtown. It woke me up."

"Go back to sleep!" he said. "It can't be anything."

"No," she said, "I'm frightened. I wonder what it is. I wonder if the baby has enough covers." The wailing was still going on. "It couldn't be an air-raid warning, could it?"

"Of course not," he said reassuringly, but she could hear the indecision in his voice.

"Why don't you turn on the radio," she said, "just to see? Just to make sure. I'll go and see if the baby's covered up." They walked down the hall in their pajamas. He went into the kitchen, turned on the radio, and waited for it to warm up. There was nothing but static and hum.

"What's that station?" he called to her. "Conrad, or something like that."

"That's 640 on the dial," she said, from the baby's room. He twisted the dial and suddenly the radio screamed at him, frightening him badly.

"*This is not an exercise. This is not an exercise. This is not an exercise,*" the radio blared. "*This is an air-raid warning. This is an air-raid warning. We will be attacked in fifteen minutes. We will be attacked in fifteen minutes. This is not an exercise.*" He recognized the voice of a local announcer who did an hour of breakfast music daily. He had never heard the man talk like that before. He ran into the baby's room while the radio shrieked behind him: "*We will be attacked in fifteen minutes. Correction. Correction. In fourteen minutes. In fourteen minutes. We will be at-*

tacked in fourteen minutes. This is not an exercise."

"Look," he said, "don't ask me any questions, please, just do exactly what I tell you and don't waste any time." She stared at him with her mouth open. "Listen," he said, "and do exactly as I say. They say this is an air-raid and we'd better believe them." She looked frightened nearly out of her wits. "I'll look after you," he said; "just get dressed as fast as you can. Put on as many layers of wool as you can. Get that?"

She nodded speechlessly.

"Put on your woolen topcoat and your fur coat over that. Get as many scarves as you can find. We'll wrap our faces and hands. When you're dressed, dress the baby the same way. We have a chance, if you do as I say without wasting time." She ran off up the hall to the coat closet and he could hear her pulling things about.

"This will be an attack with nuclear weapons. You have thirteen minutes to take cover," screamed the radio. He looked at his watch and hurried to the kitchen and pulled a cardboard carton from under the sink. He threw two can openers into it and all the canned goods he could see. There were three loaves of bread in the breadbox and he crammed them into the carton. He took everything that was wrapped and solid in the refrigerator and crushed it in. When the carton was full he took a bucket which usually held a garbage bag, rinsed it hastily, and filled

it with water. There was a plastic bottle in the refrigerator. He poured the tomato juice out of it and rinsed it and filled it with water.

"*This will be a nuclear attack.*" The disc-jockey's voice was cracking with hysteria. "*You have nine minutes, nine minutes, to take cover. Nine minutes.*" He ran into the dark hall and bumped into his wife who was swaddled like a bear.

"Go and dress the baby," he said. "We're going to make it, we've just got time. I'll go and get dressed." She was crying, but there was no time for comfort. In the bedroom he forced himself into his trousers, a second pair of trousers, two shirts and two sweaters. He put on the heaviest, loosest jacket he owned, a topcoat, and finally his overcoat. This took him just under five minutes. When he rejoined his wife in the living room, she had the baby swaddled in her arms, still asleep.

"Go to the back room in the cellar, where your steamer trunk is," he said, "and take this." He gave her a flashlight which they kept in their bedroom. When she hesitated he said roughly, "Go on, get going."

"Aren't you coming?"

"Of course I'm coming," he said. He turned the radio up as far as it would go and noted carefully what the man said. "*This will be a nuclear attack. The target will probably be the aircraft company. You have three minutes to take cover.*" He picked up the carton and balanced the bottle of water on it. With the other hand he carried the bucket. Leaving the kitchen door wide open, he went to the cellar, passed through the dark furnace room, and joined his wife.

"Put out the flashlight," he said. "We'll have to save it. We have a minute or two, so listen to me." They could hear the radio upstairs. *"Two minutes,"* it screamed.

"Lie down in the corner of the west and north walls," he said quickly. "The blast should come from the north if they hit the target, and the house will blow down and fall to the south. Lie on top of the baby and I'll lie on top of you!"

She cuddled the sleeping infant in her arms. "We're going to die right now," she said, as she held the baby closer to her.

"No, we aren't," he said, "we have a chance. Wrap the scarves around your face and the baby's, and lie down." She handed him a plaid woolen scarf and he tied it around his face so that only his eyes showed. He placed the water and food in a corner and then lay down on top of his wife, spreading his arms and legs as much as possible, to cover and protect her.

"Twenty seconds," shrieked the radio. *"Eighteen seconds. Fifteen."*

He looked at his watch as he fell. "Ten seconds," he said aloud. "It's five o'clock. They won't waste a megaton bomb on us. They'll save it for New York." They heard the radio crackle into silence and they hung onto each other, keeping their eyes closed tightly.

Instantaneously the cellar room lit up with a kind of glow they had never seen before, the

earthen floor began to rock and heave, and
the absolutely unearthly sound began. There
was no way of telling how far off it was, the
explosion. The sound seemed to be inside
them, in their bowels; the very air itself was
shattered and blown away in the dreadful
sound that went on and on and on.

They held their heads down, hers pushed
into the dirt, shielding the baby's scalp, his
face crushed into her hair, nothing of their
skin exposed to the glow, and the sound went
on and on, pulsing curiously, louder than anything they had ever imagined, louder than
deafening, quaking in their eardrums, louder
and louder until it seemed that what had exploded was there in the room on top of them
in a blend of smashed, torn air, cries of the
instantly dead, fall of steel, timber, and brick,
crash of masonry and glass — they couldn't
sort any of it out — all were there, all imagi-
nable noises of destruction synthesized. It was
like absolutely nothing they had ever heard
before and it so filled their skulls, pushing outward from the brainpan, that they could not
divide it into its parts. All that they could
understand, if they understood anything, was
that this was the ultimate catastrophe, and
that they were still recording it, expecting any
second to be crushed into blackness, but as
long as they were recording it they were still
living. They felt, but did not think, this. They
only understood it instinctively and held on
tighter to each other, waiting for the smash,
the crush, the black.

But it became lighter and lighter, the glow in the cellar room, waxing and intensifying itself. It had no color that they recognized through their tightly-shut eyelids. It might have been called green, but it was not green, nor any neighbor of green. Like the noise, it was a dreadful compound of ultimately destructive fire, blast, terrible energy released from a bursting sun, like the birth of the solar system. Incandescence beyond an infinite number of lights swirled around them.

The worst was the nauseous rocking to and fro of the very earth beneath them, worse than an earthquake, which might have seemed reducible to human dimensions, those of some disaster witnessed in the movies or on television. But this was no gaping, opening seam in the earth, but a threatened total destruction of the earth itself, right to its core, a pulverization of the world. They tried like animals to scrabble closer and closer in under the north cellar wall even as they expected it to fall on them. They kept their heads down, waiting for death to take them as it had taken their friends, neighbors, fellow workers, policemen, firemen, soldiers; and the dreadful time passed and still they did not die in the catastrophe. And they began to sense obscurely that the longer they were left uncrushed, the better grew their chances of survival. And pitifully, slowly their feelings began to resume their customary segmented play amongst themselves, while the event was still unfolding. They could not help doing the characteristic, the human thing, the beginning to think and struggle to live.

Through their shut eyelids the light began to seem less incandescent, more recognizably a color familiar to human beings and less terrifying because it might be called a hue of green instead of no-color-at-all. It became green, still glowing and illuminating the cellar like daylight, but anyway green, nameable as such and therefore familiar and less dreadful. The light grew more and more darkly green in an insane harmony with the rocking and the sound.

As the rocking slowed, as they huddled closer and closer in under the north foundation, a split in the cellar wall showed itself almost in front of their hidden faces, and yet the wall stood and did not come in on top of them. It held and, holding, gave them more chance for survival although they didn't know it. The earth's upheaval slowed and sank back and no gaps appeared in the earth under them, no crevasse to swallow them up under the alteration of the earth's crust. And in time the rocking stopped and the floor of their world was still, but they would not move, afraid to move a limb for fear of being caught in the earth's mouth.

The noise continued, but began to distinguish itself in parts, and the worst, basic element attenuated itself; that terrible crash apart of the atmosphere under the bomb had stopped by now, the atmosphere had parted to admit the ball of radioactivity, had been blown hundreds of miles in every direction and had rushed back to regain its place, disputing the place with the ball of radioactivity, so that there grew up a thousand-mile vortex of cyclonic winds around the hub of the displacement. The cyclone was almost comforting, sounding, whistling, in whatever stood upright, not trees certainly, but tangled steel beams and odd bits of masonry. The sound of these winds came to them in the cellar. Soon they were able to name sounds, and distinguish them from others which they heard, mainly sounds of fire — no sounds of the dying, no human cries at all, no sounds of life. Only the fires and cyclonic winds.

Now they could feel, and hear enough to shout to each other over the fire and wind.

The man tried to stir, to ease his wife's position. He could move his torso as far as the waist or perhaps the hips. Below that, although he was in no pain and not paralyzed, he was immobilized by a heavy weight. He could feel his legs and feet; they were sound and unhurt, but he could not move them. He waited, lying there trying to sort things out, until some sort of ordered thought and some communication was possible, when the noise should lessen sufficiently. He could hear his wife shouting something into the dirt in front of her face and he tried to make it out.

"She slept through it," he heard, "she slept through it," and he couldn't believe it, although it was true. The baby lived and recollected none of the horror.

"She slept through it," screamed the wife idiotically, "she's still asleep." It couldn't be true, he thought, it was impossible, but there was no way to check her statement until they could move about. The baby must have been three feet below the blast and the glow, shielded by a two-and-a-half-foot wall of flesh, his and his wife's, and the additional thickness of layers of woolen clothing. She should certainly have survived, if they had, but how could she have slept through the noise, the awful light, and the rocking? He listened and waited, keeping his head down and his face covered.

Supposing that they had survived the initial blast, as seemed to be the case; there was still the fallout to consider. The likelihood, he thought (he was beginning to be able to think) was that they were already being eaten up by radiation and would soon die of monstrous cancers, or plain, simple leukemia, or rottenness of the cortex. It was miraculous that they had lived through the first shock; they could hardly hope that their luck would hold through the later dangers. He thought that the baby might not have been infected so far, shielded as she was, and he began to wonder how she might be helped to evade death from radiation in the next few days. Let her live a week, he thought, and she may go on living into the next generation, if there is one.

Nothing would be the same in the next generation; there would be few people and fewer laws, the national boundaries would have perished — there would be a new world to invent. Somehow the child must be preserved for that, even if their own lives were to be forfeited immediately. He felt perfectly healthy so far, untouched by any creeping sickness as he lay there, forcing himself and the lives beneath him deeper into their burrow. He began to make plans; there was nothing else for him to do, just then.

The noise of the winds had become regular now and the green glow had subsided; the earth was still and they were still together and in the same place, in their cellar, in their home. He thought of his books, his checkbook, his phonograph records, his wife's household appliances. They were gone, of course, which didn't matter. What mattered was that the way they had lived was gone, the whole texture of their habits. The city would be totally uninhabitable. If they were to survive longer, they must get out of the city at once. They would have to decide immediately when they should try to leave the city, and they must keep themselves alive until that time.

"What time is it?" gasped his wife from below him in a tone pitched in almost her normal voice. He was relieved to hear her speak in the commonplace, familiar tone; he had been afraid that hysteria and shock would destroy their personalities all at once. So far they had held together. Later on, when the loss of their whole world sank in, when they appreciated the full extent of their losses, they would run the risk of insanity or, at the least, extreme neurotic disturbance. But right now they could converse, calculate, and wait for the threat of madness to appear days, or years, later.

He looked at his watch. "Eight-thirty," he said. Everything had ended in three-and-a-half hours. "Are you all right?" he asked.

"I think so," she said, "I don't feel any pain and the baby's fine. She's warm and she doesn't seem frightened."

He tried to move his legs and was relieved to see that they answered the nervous impulse. He lifted his head fearfully and twisted it around to see behind him. His legs were buried under a pile of loose brick and rubble which grew smaller toward his thighs; his torso was quite uncovered. "I'm all right," he said, beginning to work his legs free; they were undoubtedly badly bruised, but they didn't seem to be crushed or broken; at the worst he might have torn muscles or a bad sprain. He had to be very careful, he reasoned, as he worked at his legs. He might dislodge something and bring the remnant of the house down around them. Very, very slowly he lifted his torso by doing a push-up with his arms. His wife slid out from underneath, pushing the baby in front of her. When she was free she laid the child gently to one side, whispering to her and promising her food. She crawled around to her husband's side and began to push the bricks off his legs.

"Be careful," he whispered. "Take them as

they come. Don't be in too much of a hurry."

She nodded, picking out the bricks gingerly, but as fast as she could. Soon he was able to roll over on his back and sit up. By a quarter to ten he was free and they took time to eat and drink. The three of them sat together in a cramped, narrow space under the cellar beams, perhaps six feet high and six or seven feet square. They were getting air from somewhere although it might be deadly air, and there was no smell of gas. He had been afraid that they might be suffocated in their shelter.

"Do you suppose the food's contaminated?" she asked.

"What if it is?" he said. "So are we, just as much as the food. There's nothing to do but risk it. Only be careful what you give the baby."

"How can I tell?"

"I don't know," he said. "Say a prayer and trust in God." He found the flashlight, which had rolled into a corner, and tried it. It worked very well.

"What are we going to do? We can't stay here."

"I don't even know for sure that we can get out," he said, "but we'll try. There should be a window just above us that leads to a crawl-space under the patio. That's one of the reasons why I told you to come here. In any case we'd be wise to stay here for a few hours until the very worst of the fallout is down."

"What'll we do when we get out?"

"Try to get out of town. Get our outer clothes off, get them all off for that matter, and scrub ourselves with water. Maybe we can get to the river."

"Why don't you try the window right now so we can tell whether we can get out?"

"I will as soon as I've finished eating and had a rest. My legs are very sore."

He could hear her voice soften. "Take your time," she said.

When he felt rested, he stood up. He could almost stand erect and with the flashlight was able to find the window quickly. It was level with his face. He piled loose bricks against the wall below it and climbed up on them until the window was level with his chest. Knocking out the screen with the butt of the flashlight, he put his head through and then flashed the light around; there were no obstructions that he could see, and he couldn't smell anything noxious. The patio, being a flat, level space, had evidently been swept clean by the blast without being flattened. They could crawl out of the cellar under the patio, he realized, and then kick a hole in the lath and stucco which skirted it.

He stepped down from the pile of brick and told his wife that they would be able to get out whenever they wished, that the crawl space was clear.

"What time is it?"

"Half-past twelve."

"Should we try it now?"

"I think so," he said. "At first I thought we

ought to stay here for a day or two, but now I think we ought to try and get out from under the fallout. We may have to walk a couple of hundred miles."

"We can do it," she said and he felt glad. She had always been able to look unpleasant issues in the face.

He helped her through the cellar window and handed up the baby, who clucked and chuckled when he spoke to her. He pushed the carton of food and the bucket of water after them. Then he climbed up and they inched forward under the patio.

"I hear a motor," said his wife suddenly.

He listened and heard it too.

"Looking for survivors," he said eagerly. "Probably the Army or Civil Defense. Come on."

He swung himself around on his hips and back and kicked out with both feet at the lath and stucco. Three or four kicks did it. His wife went first, inching the baby through the hole. He crawled after her into the daylight; it looked like any other day except that the city was leveled. The sky and the light were the same; everything else was gone. They sat up, muddy, scratched, nervously exhausted, in a ruined flower bed. Not fifty feet away stood an olive-drab truck, the motor running loudly. Men shouted to them.

"Come on, you!" shouted the men in the truck. "Get going!" They stood and ran raggedly to the cab, she holding the child and he their remaining food and water. In the cab was a canvas-sheeted, goggled driver, peering at them through huge eyes. "Get in the back," he ordered. "We've got to get out right away. Too hot." They climbed into the truck and it began to move instantly.

"Army Survival Unit," said a goggled and hooded man in the back of the truck. "Throw away that food and water; it's dangerous. Get your outer clothing off quick. Throw it out!" They obeyed him without thinking, stripping off their loose outer clothes and dropping them out of the truck.

"You're the only ones we've found in a hundred city blocks," said the soldier. "Did you know the war's over? There's a truce."

"Who won?"

"Over in half an hour," he said, "and nobody won."

"What are you going to do with us?"

"Drop you at a check-out point forty miles from here. Give you the scrub-down treatment, wash off the fallout. Medical check for radiation sickness. Clean clothes. Then we send you on your way to a refugee station."

"How many died?"

"Everybody in the area. Almost no exceptions. You're a statistic, that's what you are. Must have been a fluke of the blast."

"Will we live?"

"Sure you will. You're living now, aren't you?"

"I guess so," he said.

"Sure you'll live! Maybe not too long. But

everybody else is dead! And you'll be taken care of." He fell silent.

They looked at each other, determined to live as long as they could. The wife cuddled her child close against her thin silk blouse. For a long time they jolted along over rocks and broken pavement without speaking. When the pavement smoothed out the husband knew that they must be out of the disaster area. In a few more minutes they were out of immediate danger; they had reached the check-out point. It was a quarter to three in the afternoon.

"Out you get," said the soldier. "We've got to go back." They climbed out of the truck and he handed down the baby. "You're all right now," he said. "Good luck."

"Good-bye," they said.

The truck turned about and drove away and they turned silently, hand in hand, and walked toward the medical tents. They were the seventh, eighth, and ninth living persons to be brought there after the sirens.

The Spaceman Cometh

HENRY GREGOR FELSEN

He's an alien who came to Earth, married one of the "locals," and raised a regular Iowa family. He loves his peaceful life and dreads being discovered by his people, the Adnaxians. Adnaxians bomb planets *first* and ask questions second. So when an Adnaxian saucer dropped from the sky, he knew dramatic measures were called for.

I was trying to compose the speech I was to make at our town assembly, and like most writers I was gazing out of the window looking for inspiration in the sky. I was looking at a small white cloud when an Adnaxian flying saucer sailed across my line of vision and disappeared in the direction of Razza's Woods.

Although I now live in Center Valley, Iowa, with my Earthborn wife and two children, and I have assumed the disguise of a middle-aged male human, I was born on the planet Adnaxas and lived there for several hundred Earth-years. When I was forced to flee my home planet several Earth-years ago, I escaped in a space ship that I stole from the Adnaxian Air Force. That's why I know what it was I saw.

It was no accident that the Adnaxian pilot was heading for Razza's Woods. I had parked my old flying saucer out there at treetop level, and although I had rendered it invisible to human eyes, I knew the saucerman must have spotted it and was coming down to investigate.

I had a great and terrible feeling of despair.

Until this moment I had been certain that I was the only Adnaxian who knew about Earth. I had first come here to scout Earth for destruction, but to use an old Adnaxian expression, I had goofed. I happened to fall in love with a girl I met in a drugstore.

Because of that and certain difficulties I encountered when I returned to Adnaxas to make my report, I had fled back to Earth, married the girl, and settled down to a quiet life in a small town.

But now the Earth had been discovered by another Adnaxian, and I knew too well what that meant. The pilot would return to Adnaxas with his report. Within hours there would be a fleet of bombers on their way through space. For it has always been the Adnaxian custom, when a new planet is discovered, to destroy the planet before it can commit an act of aggression. After that a team of scientists is put to work examining the planet fragments to determine whether it would have been a hostile or a friendly planet.

My duty was clear. Somehow I had to prevent the saucerman from returning to Adnaxas, so that the existence and location of Earth would remain unknown to my ruthless home planet.

But how?

My minds, conscious, subconscious, and Adnaxian, refused to function. The only plan that came to me was to surrender myself, start back toward Adnaxas with the saucerman, and somehow destroy him and myself before we reached that planet. The thought of leaving my wife and children forever made me so unhappy I groaned aloud.

"Is something wrong, dear? Are you ill?"

I turned. My wife was standing in the doorway, a look of concern on her face and a dustcloth in her hand.

"I'm all right," I said mournfully. "It's this speech I have to make." I seized this lie and went on bravely, "I can't think of any ideas. I think I'll take a little walk. I might get an idea that way."

"I'm sure you'll think of something," my wife said. "A good long walk will clear your head. Sitting in here and smoking so much, no wonder you can't think."

I went to her and took her in my arms. "Good-bye, darling," I said, trying to keep my voice under control. I gave her a last, long, loving kiss.

"Where are the children?" I asked quietly. "I'd like to say good-bye to them too."

"What's the matter with you?" my wife asked. "You're only going for a little walk. The way you act, one would think you were taking a trip to the moon."

The moon — when I reached that satellite my trip would just have started. But my wife thought I was an Earthman, and this was no time to explain that for the last ten years she had been married to a being from outer space, and that I was leaving her in order to save the world. I mean, you just can't come out and tell your wife something like that after ten years. Chances are she wouldn't believe half of it.

I sighed and said the last Earthwords that would ever pass my lips: "Yes, dear." Then I left the house and began my tragic journey out of this world.

"Take your hat!" my wife shouted after me. "If you go walking around bareheaded, I'm the one who has to listen to your complaining about your sinus trouble!"

I pretended not to hear her and went off thinking bitter thoughts. What an inglorious beginning to a mission whose goal was the salvation of Earth. I was willing to make the sacrifice, but how awful that I could tell no one, not even my wife. I had to walk away from my loved ones as though for a little while, and never return. They would wait, wonder, worry, and finally decide I had deserted them. In time I would be declared dead, my children would be grown, and my wife married to someone else. When I was thought of, it would be unkindly. Take my hat? It was a new hat, and expensive. Better to leave it. Perhaps it would fit the head of her next husband. It was the least I could do.

When I reached Razza's Woods, I took one last human look around, then reverted to my Adnaxian shape, which made me invisible to Earthmen's eyes. As I did so I was seized by the most terrible pains, and I was terrified by a tearing sound that seemed to come from my body. And then, suddenly, I felt better. I looked down at myself and understood. Ten years of good Earth home cooking had taken their toll, and I had outgrown my old Adnaxian Air Force uniform. The sudden change had popped my buttons and split my trousers. I sighed, and lost another button.

I had little time to mourn that which had once been my dashing figure. I heard blasts from a couple of shotguns — they couldn't have been more than a few hundred yards away — and at almost the same moment the Adnaxian saucer skimmed over my head and came to rest in the clearing where I stood. The moment it touched Earth the pilot rendered it invisible to human eyes.

I heard excited voices and the sound of men crashing through the brush. In a moment Dave Nichols and Jack Wilson burst into the clearing carrying their guns and looking eagerly from side to side.

"He fell right in here," Dave shouted. "I got him with both barrels, Biggest damn' Canada goose you ever saw!"

"Canada goose my foot," Jack said. "I hit him after you missed, and it was a big canvasback duck. I saw those markings as clear as anything."

"Well, he ain't here," David said. "And we'd better keep looking. He won't go far with my lead in him."

"*Your* lead!" Jack yelled. "You mean *my* lead."

Arguing violently, my two neighbors moved on. The hatch on the saucer opened slowly and the saucerman looked around cautiously. Then he stepped out, clutching an Adnaxian molecule pistol in one hand and a thick briefcase in the other.

Knowing that one burst from the pistol could destroy the whole county, I hurried forward. "Don't shoot!" I cried in Adnaxian.

The saucerman aimed his pistol at me. "Don't shoot," I repeated. "I am one of you."

The saucerman lowered the pistol which, I now saw, he was holding by the wrong end. "Eureka!" he exclaimed. "I have found you! Squadron Leader Ex-my-ex, I presume?"

"Yes," I said. "I am Ex-my-ex."

The saucerman looked at my tattered uniform and potbelly. "You've changed," he said a little sadly, putting away his pistol. "But then, I suppose it's a wonder you're alive at all, exiled here millions of light years away from civilization. Don't you know me?"

I looked at him closely. "The pseudopodia are familiar, but I can't remember the name," I said lamely.

"My-ex-ex," he said. "University of Adnaxas. You were a student of mine in cosmichemistry."

"Of course," I said. "Now I remember. But what are you doing here, sir?"

"Looking for you, by order of the Presidex," he said. "He's quite anxious to get you back."

I shuddered. I had seen what happened to Adnaxians who has displeased the Presidex.

"When you fled," My-ex-ex went on, "popular opinion held that you were lost forever in space. But a few of us felt that you actually had a remote planet tucked up your sleeve. After the military gave up the search, some of us scientists were given the job of finding you. Since I knew you personally, I was chosen to make the first search-flight. And I seem to have found you. Stroke of luck, that, what?"

"For you," I said resignedly. "I'll return with you, sir. I suppose we might as well start back now." I was ready. The sooner we started, the sooner I could destroy us both in space.

"That's not possible," Professor My-ex-ex said, parting his briefcase. "My orders were, if I found you on a new planet, to investigate the planet and bring back a complete report for the Presidex — so he'll know how to deal with the new planet, you know."

I knew. Hadn't I "dealt" with other planets myself? I'd destroyed fourteen singlehanded before fleeing Adnaxas. And now, Earth was next.

But there was a ray of hope. Professor My-ex-ex had always been a good sort, a little vague at times, but kind. If I could show him what a fine place Earth was, and how nice the people were, and let him see the peaceful charm of my family life, perhaps he would be moved to pity and spare us. Perhaps he would allow me to remain on Earth, and not even report Earth's existence to Adnaxas. It was worth a try. If I failed, there was always the violent ending in midspace.

"Now," Professor My-ex-ex said briskly, "I trust you will assist me in my mission, which was communicated to me orally by the Secretary of Space. I can put in a good word for you when we return to Adnaxas, you know."

"I am yours to command, sir," I said, beginning my campaign to make him think kindly of Earth.

"Good. Now, since you have managed to survive on this planet for some time, I take it you have had some contact with the natives."

"Oh, yes," I said. "I not only assumed their form, but I married a local girl, and — "

"You *went native?*" Professor My-ex-ex looked at me disapprovingly.

"Yes, sir," I admitted, blushing. "I married a native girl and we have a family. After all, sir, I thought I would be here for life."

"Don't apologize, lad," Professor My-ex-ex said archly. "I'm not surprised. I know you Air Force chaps. Who else could dash off blindly into space, travel a million light years, and wind up on a planet with girls? You rascal! I'd like to study your family. Could it be arranged without their knowing who I am?"

"Oh, sure," I said. "Change yourself into human form and I'll introduce you as an old friend from Brooklyn. Then, no matter what you say, no one will think you strange. I'll change into human form first, to show you what Earth-people look like."

I changed back to my usual human form. The professor watched me closely, chuckling to himself and making notes for future lectures — and scolding himself because he had forgotten to bring along a camera. "I think I have it," he said, stepping back. "Join you in a moment, my boy."

A moment later he stood before me in human form. It was a fairly normal example of a human, vaguely familiar. I took a second, closer, look. The professor had changed himself to look exactly like me.

"Begging your pardon, sir," I said, "but you look exactly like me."

"Yes. Good job of copying, what?"

"But, sir," I said patiently, "it's awkward. It would be better if you changed to look like some other human."

Professor My-ex-ex stared. "What do you mean, Ex-my-ex?" he asked. "Don't all humans look alike?"

"No, sir," I said. "Except for twins and such, no two humans look alike."

"By Presidex, man!" the professor exclaimed. "If they all look different, how do they recognize one another?"

"You have to remember each face, and whose it is," I said.

"I've never heard of such chaos," the professor sputtered. "Now up on Adnaxas, where everyone looks exactly alike, you look at a fellow and you *know* him. But when no two look alike that's nothing but reproductive anarchy. Very sloppy ethnogeny in *my* book, young man."

"Just give us time, sir," I said. "We're a young planet here, and not too polished as yet, but we're making progress. Why, only yesterday I saw two women wearing identical hats and they had identical looks on their faces."

The professor said something under his breath and changed again. This time he appeared as the human equivalent of what he was in Adnaxian form. He turned out to be a hesitant, elderly gentleman with thick glasses, a small, ragged mustache, an unpressed tweed suit, and a black Homburg. The briefcase remained unchanged. We decided to call him George Hoskins.

"Tell me, Henry," Professor Hoskins said as we set out for town, "just what sort of place is this planet?"

"Earth's a great little planet, sir," I said. "Plenty of schools, churches, shopping, and transportation, and growing by leaps and bounds. It's been a real home away from home for me, sir, and I've grown to love the place."

"What is the temper of the natives?"

"Friendly as all outdoors," I said. "That's the very hallmark of an Earthman, sir. The desire for friendship and peace."

"Well," the professor said, frowning, "just before I landed I heard several explosions, and a number of pellets came through the hull of my saucer, narrowly missing my *Kopf.* Is that the usual greeting your earth-guards give a visitor from another planet?"

I laughed. "That wasn't the military firing at you, sir," I said. "A couple of my neighbors thought you were a wild fowl."

"One of the enemies of the human?"

"Oh, no," I said. "Wild fowl are plump, harmless birds about the size of your brief-case. They couldn't hurt a human."

"Why do humans shoot them?"

"For sport and fun," I began. "It's quite a thrill to — " The look on the professor's face stopped me. What a way I had chosen to impress him with the peacefulness of the human! "It's not *all* sport," I said quickly. "The hunters eat the birds they kill."

"How revolting," the professor said. "So Earthmen are friendly and peaceful, are they?"

"Well," I said, "yes, they are. You'll see. We're not a hostile people, sir." We had arrived in town now. "Earthmen are just plain folks, who believe we ought to live and let — *look out, sir!*"

The professor had stepped off a curb without looking once in either direction. I grabbed him by the arm just in time to pull him from the path of a hot rod that was tearing past us.

"My word!" the professor cried, fumbling for his molecule pistol. "We are being attacked!"

"Please calm yourself, sir," I said. "There's nothing to be alarmed about. That was just one of the high school boys on his way home in his car."

Professor My-ex-ex looked at me strangely. "You mean there was a *child* in control of that machine? Is it normal on Earth to allow children to destroy others at will?"

"Oh, no," I said, "they don't *try* to kill anyone. If they do, it goes hard with the parents. It's the children's way of having a little fun."

"I am beginning to dread the sound of that word," Professor My-ex-ex said. "Tell me, if human men shoot everything that moves, and human children run over everything that doesn't, how is it there are any humans left alive?"

I'm sure there's an answer, but I couldn't think of it.

Professor My-ex-ex looked quite unhappy by now and I was worried. I decided to stop off at the Town Club and show him how friendly men really are. I explained that the club was a place where men of good will and similar tastes gathered to enjoy one another's company and conversation.

The moment we entered, we ran into Big Bud Taplinger, one of our heartiest members.

When I introduced George Hoskins to Big Bud, my large neighbor was delighted to meet my old friend.

"It's a real pleasure to meet you, George!" Big Bud roared, squeezing the professor's hand until the bones cracked. "Put 'er there!" Big Bud pumped the professor's arm with violent good will and clapped him on the back so hard that he knocked the poor old saucer-man against the bar.

"Big Bud likes you," I whispered to My-ex-ex as I handed him back his glasses. "You'll like him too. He's the kindest-hearted, friend-liest man you'll find on Earth."

"He is?" My-ex-ex gasped. "Presidex help me!"

I wanted My-ex-ex to stay and have a drink, but he insisted we leave at once. Perhaps it was better that way.

As we approached my house we heard a series of shrill cries and several small figures in space helmets dashed toward us, firing their weapons wildly, and dropping dead only to bounce up again and continue the battle.

"The Moogislanders!" My-ex-ex cried, reaching frantically for his molecule pistol. "Run for your life!"

"It's all right, sir," I said soothingly. "It's just the children playing war."

"Children? Playing *war?*"

"It's their favorite game," I said. "As long as they get a lot of fun — "

"That *word,*" My-ex-ex groaned. "I must

make a note of this custom. Children, playing *war!*"

"They don't really kill anyone," I said. "It's a harmless way of letting off steam, and the psychologists say that children who play out their fears — "

We were interrupted by two of the children, who got into a fist fight over possession of a gun. Both ran off crying, and the scratches I got from separating them hardly bled at all.

We went inside and I introduced My-ex-ex to my wife, telling her he was staying for dinner.

My wife gave My-ex-ex the big welcome, assured him he would be no trouble at all, kissed me while he beamed at us, and bit me the moment he looked away. If I hadn't screamed in pain, he might never have noticed.

"Affectionate little woman," I said, laughing painfully as I led My-ex-ex into the living room.

"Yes, indeed," he said warily. "Hope she doesn't take too much of a liking to me. I bruise easily."

We sat down in the living room and turned on the TV set. "This is the way the Earthman likes to live," I said to My-ex-ex. "Snug in his little home; with his wife and children, quietly watching the programs of entertainment and education that are on television. The children's programs are on now, but later you'll be able to get a better idea of our cultural values."

The kids came in and sat down to watch with us, and for the next two hours we were treated to a succession of cowboy adventures that filled the room with the thunder of hoofs, the roar of guns, and the thud of fists on flesh. We saw men shot, stabbed, trampled by wild horses. By the time the children's programs had ended, our little ones had gone to sleep and My-ex-ex was a nervous wreck.

We had dinner in front of the television set, and watched as the cowboys and space thrillers gave way to the crime stories. We were treated to the more refined forms of violence, sadism, and mayhem.

All during these programs My-ex-ex kept making notes and shaking his head. I had the idea that he, being a stranger, failed to appreciate the cozy warmth and peaceful affection of family life — especially when I had to spank the children so they would go to bed.

My-ex-ex's dour expression didn't change until my mother-in-law arrived after dinner. My mother-in-law is a handsome, silver-haired woman and two minutes after she arrived, My-ex-ex was scurrying around getting her an ash tray, lighting her cigarette, and making little jokes. When I saw how well the two of them were getting along, I felt the first real ray of hope for the future of Earth. Might it not turn out that the mother would save Earth as once the daughter had?

Everything went along beautifully for a while. My-ex-ex was discoursing learnedly on a theory of cosmichemical philology, and Mother-in-law was nodding her head, sipping tea as she listened. The fire on the hearth crackled, and there was an air of good cheer, comfort, and love in our house. My-ex-ex had put away his notebook and was flirting with my mother-in-law.

Then came wrestling.

My-ex-ex stared in hurt disbelief as my mother-in-law turned her back on him and leaned toward the television screen. He was about to continue his discussion when the Gorilla Kid got the anaconda hold on Elegant Eddie.

"Tear his arm off!" my mother-in-law screamed. "Break his back!"

My-ex-ex watched as the wrestlers gouged, kicked, and twisted. His eyes were as big as teacups. "Wrestling," I whispered to him. "The women love to watch it, even if it isn't more than a farce."

"Beat his head against the post!" my mother-in-law screamed.

Professor My-ex-ex stood up. "I think I'll lie down for a while," he said weakly. Avoiding my mother-in-law's flailing fists, My-ex-ex went into the guest room and closed the door.

I waited a while, and when I heard no sound I went into the guest room to investigate. The room was empty, and the window was open. My heart stood still. My-ex-ex had fled. He was on his way to Adnaxas, and it was too late to stop him. We were doomed!

A piece of paper on the dresser caught my eye, and I read the message on it, written in a scholarly hand:

> *Dear Ex-my-ex,*
> *I am returning to Adnaxas. I have been horrified by the violence of humans, and terrified by their idea of fun. I offer you this promise. I will never mention Earth on Adnaxas if you will never let Earth know there is such a planet as Adnaxas. Since you fled we have a new Presidex and live peaceful, quiet lives. I shudder to think what our dear planet would be like if Earthmen ever found it and moved in. Good-bye forever. Regards to your family.*
>
> *My-ex-ex*

I read the message over and over. We were safe! Safe!

I went back into the living room. My wife and my mother-in-law were sitting quietly, now that the wrestling was over. They were talking about the price of yard goods.

"Where is your friend Professor Hoskins?" my mother-in-law asked me.

"He had to leave during the wrestling," I said. "He asked me to say good-bye to you."

"He was a nice little man," my mother-in-law said. "But he must have had his nose in a book all his life. I don't think that man ever went anywhere or did anything."

"By the way," my wife said to me. "Do you have your speech ready for the town assembly?"

I shook my head. "Can't think of an idea," I said helplessly.

"Well," my wife said, "the kids are all so crazy about science fiction, and you read it all the time yourself, why not give a talk telling why it is impossible to travel between planets?"

"Darling," I said, "that's a wonderful suggestion. It's time we talked about space travel in terms of cold facts instead of fiction. I'm just the man to prove it can't be done."

The Nine Billion Names of God

ARTHUR C. CLARKE

High up in their remote mountain monastery, devout monks have been working for years, patiently compiling lists of all the possible names of God. With the installation of the Automatic Sequence Computer, their work has been greatly simplified. Now, the list can be completed in one hundred days rather than 15,000 years. But then what happens? The two American computer specialists are suddenly very apprehensive.

"This is a slightly unusual request," said Dr. Wagner, with what he hoped was commendable restraint. "As far as I know, it's the first time anyone's been asked to supply a Tibetan monastery with an Automatic Sequence Computer. I don't wish to be inquisitive, but I should hardly have thought that your — ah — establishment had much use for such a machine. Could you explain just what you intend to do with it?"

"Gladly," replied the lama, readjusting his silk robes and carefully putting away the slide rule he had been using for currency conversions. "Your Mark V Computer can carry out any routine mathematical operation involving up to ten digits. However, for our work we are interested in *letters*, not numbers. As we wish you to modify the output circuits, the machine will be printing words, not columns of figures."

"I don't quite understand. . . ."

"This is a project on which we have been working for the last three centuries — since the lamasery was founded, in fact. It is somewhat alien to your way of thought, so I hope you will listen with an open mind while I explain it."

"Naturally."

"It is really quite simple. We have been compiling a list which shall contain all the possible names of God."

"I beg your pardon?"

"We have reason to believe," continued the lama imperturbably, "that all such names can be written with not more than nine letters in an alphabet we have devised."

"And you have been doing this for three centuries?"

"Yes: we expected it would take us about fifteen thousand years to complete the task."

"Oh," Dr. Wagner looked a little dazed. "Now I see why you wanted to hire one of our machines. But exactly what is the *purpose* of this project?"

The lama hesitated for a fraction of a second, and Wagner wondered if he had offended him. If so, there was no trace of annoyance in the reply.

"Call it ritual, if you like, but it's a fundamental part of our belief. All the many names of the Supreme Being — God, Jehovah, Allah, and so on — they are only man-made labels. There is a philosophical problem of some difficulty here, which I do not propose to discuss, but somewhere among all the possible combinations of letters that can occur are what one may call the *real* names of God. By systematic permutation of letters, we have been trying to list them all."

"I see. You've been starting at AAAAAAA . . . and working up to ZZZZZZZ. . . ."

"Exactly — though we use a special alphabet of our own. Modifying the electromatic typewriters to deal with this is, of course, trivial. A rather more interesting problem is that of devising suitable circuits to eliminate ridiculous combinations. For example, no letter must occur more than three times in succession."

"Three? Surely you mean two."

"Three is correct: I am afraid it would take too long to explain why, even if you understood our language."

"I'm sure it would," said Wagner hastily. "Go on."

"Luckily, it will be a simple matter to adapt

your Automatic Sequence Computer for this work, since once it has been programed properly it will permute each letter in turn and print the result. What would have taken us fifteen thousand years it will be able to do in a hundred days."

Dr. Wagner was scarcely conscious of the faint sounds from the Manhattan streets far below. He was in a different world, a world of natural, not man-made, mountains. High up in their remote aeries these monks had been patiently at work, generation after generation, compiling their lists of meaningless words. Was there any limit to the follies of mankind? Still, he must give no hint of his inner thoughts. The customer was always right. . . .

"There's no doubt," replied the doctor, "that we can modify the Mark V to print lists of this nature. I'm much more worried about the problem of installation and maintenance. Getting out to Tibet, in these days, is not going to be easy."

"We can arrange that. The components are small enough to travel by air — that is one reason why we chose your machine. If you can get them to India, we will provide transport from there."

"And you want to hire two of our engineers?"

"Yes, for the three months that the project should occupy."

"I've no doubt that Personnel can manage that." Dr. Wagner scribbled a note on his desk pad. "There are just two other points — "

Before he could finish the sentence the lama had produced a small slip of paper.

"This is my certified credit balance at the Asiatic Bank."

"Thank you. It appears to be — ah — adequate. The second matter is so trivial that I hesitate to mention it — but it's surprising how often the obvious gets overlooked. What source of electrical energy have you?"

"A diesel generator providing fifty kilowatts at a hundred and ten volts. It was installed about five years ago and is quite reliable. It's made life at the lamasery much more comfortable, but of course it was really installed to provide power for the motors driving the prayer wheels."

"Of course," echoed Dr. Wagner. "I should have thought of that."

The view from the parapet was vertiginous, but in time one gets used to anything. After three months, George Hanley was not impressed by the two-thousand-foot swoop into the abyss or the remote checkerboard of fields in the valley below. He was leaning against the wind-smoothed stones and staring morosely at the distant mountains whose names he had never bothered to discover.

This, thought George, was the craziest thing that had ever happened to him. "Project Shangri-La," some wit back at the labs had christened it. For weeks now the Mark V had been churning out acres of sheets covered with gibberish. Patiently, inexorably, the computer had been rearranging letters in all their possible combinations, exhausting each class before going on to the next. As the sheets had emerged from the electromatic typewriters, the monks had carefully cut them up and pasted them into enormous books. In another week, heaven be praised, they would have finished. Just what obscure calculations had convinced the monks that they needn't bother to go on to words of ten, twenty, or a hundred letters, George didn't know. One of his recurring nightmares was that there would be some change of plan, and that the high lama (whom they'd naturally called Sam Jaffe, though he didn't look a bit like him) would suddenly announce that the project would be extended to approximately A.D. 2060. They were quite capable of it.

George heard the heavy wooden door slam in the wind as Chuck came out onto the parapet beside him. As usual, Chuck was smoking one of the cigars that made him so popular with the monks — who, it seemed, were quite willing to embrace all the minor and most of the major pleasures of life. That was one thing in their favor: they might be crazy, but they weren't bluenoses. Those frequent trips they took down to the village, for instance . . .

"Listen, George," said Chuck urgently. "I've learned something that means trouble."

"What's wrong? Isn't the machine behaving?" That was the worst contingency George could imagine. It might delay his return, and nothing could be more horrible. The way he felt now, even the sight of a TV commercial would seem like manna from heaven. At least it would be some link with home.

"No — it's nothing like that." Chuck settled himself on the parapet, which was unusual because normally he was scared of the drop. "I've just found what all this is about."

"What d'ya mean? I thought we knew."

"Sure — we know what the monks are trying to do. But we didn't know *why*. It's the craziest thing — "

"Tell me something new," growled George.

"— but old Sam's just come clean with me. You know the way he drops in every afternoon to watch the sheets roll out. Well, this time he seemed rather excited, or at least as near as he'll ever get to it. When I told him that we were on the last cycle he asked me, in that cute English accent of his, if I'd ever wondered what they were trying to do. I said, 'Sure' — and he told me."

"Go on: I'll buy it."

"Well, they believe that when they have listed all His names — and they reckon that there are about nine billion of them — God's purpose will be achieved. The human race will have finished what it was created to do, and there won't be any point in carrying on. Indeed, the very idea is something like blasphemy."

"Then what do they expect us to do? Commit suicide?"

"There's no need for that. When the list's

completed, God steps in and simply winds things up . . . bingo!"

"Oh, I get it. When we finish our job, it will be the end of the world."

Chuck gave a nervous little laugh.

"That's just what I said to Sam. And do you know what happened? He looked at me in a very queer way, like I'd been stupid in class, and said, 'It's nothing as trivial as *that*.' "

George thought this over for a moment.

"That's what I call taking the Wide View," he said presently. "But what d'you suppose we should do about it? I don't see that it makes the slightest difference to us. After all, we already knew that they were crazy."

"Yes — but don't you see what may happen? When the list's complete and the Last Trump doesn't blow — or whatever it is they expect — *we* may get the blame. It's our machine they've been using. I don't like the situation one little bit."

"I see," said George slowly. "You've got a point there. But this sort of thing's happened before, you know. When I was a kid down in Louisiana we had a crackpot preacher who once said the world was going to end next Sunday. Hundreds of people believed him — even sold their homes. Yet when nothing happened, they didn't turn nasty, as you'd expect. They just decided that he'd made a mistake in his calculations and went right on believing. I guess some of them still do."

"Well, this isn't Louisiana, in case you

hadn't noticed. There are just two of us and hundreds of these monks. I like them, and I'll be sorry for old Sam when his lifework backfires on him. But all the same, I wish I was somewhere else."

"I've been wishing that for weeks. But there's nothing we can do until the contract's finished and the transport arrives to fly us out."

"Of course," said Chuck thoughtfully, "we could always try a bit of sabotage."

"Like hell we could! That would make things worse."

"Not the way I meant. Look at it like this. The machine will finish its run four days from now, on the present twenty-hours-a-day basis. The transport calls in a week. OK — then all we need to do is to find something that needs replacing during one of the overhaul periods — something that will hold up the works for a couple of days. We'll fix it, of course, but not too quickly. If we time matters properly, we can be down at the airfield when the last name pops out of the register. They won't be able to catch us then."

"I don't like it," said George. "It will be the first time I ever walked out on a job. Besides, it would make them suspicious. No, I'll sit tight and take what comes."

"I *still* don't like it," he said, seven days later, as the tough little mountain ponies carried them down the winding road. "And don't you think I'm running away because I'm afraid.

I'm just sorry for those poor old guys up there, and I don't want to be around when they find what suckers they've been. Wonder how Sam will take it?"

"It's funny," replied Chuck, "but when I said good-bye I got the idea he knew we were walking out on him — and that he didn't care because he knew the machine was running smoothly and that the job would soon be finished. After that — well, of course, for him there just isn't any After That. . . ."

George turned in his saddle and stared back up the mountain road. This was the last place from which one could get a clear view of the lamasery. The squat, angular buildings were silhouetted against the afterglow of the sunset: here and there, lights gleamed like portholes in the side of an ocean liner. Electric lights, of course, sharing the same circuit as the Mark V. How much longer would they share it? wondered George. Would the monks smash up the computer in their rage and disappointment? Or would they just sit down quietly and begin their calculations all over again?

He knew exactly what was happening up on the mountain at this very moment. The high lama and his assistants would be sitting in their silk robes, inspecting the sheets as the junior monks carried them away from the typewriters and pasted them into the great volumes. No one would be saying anything. The only sound would be the incessant patter, the never-ending rainstorm of the keys hitting the paper, for the Mark V itself was utterly silent as it flashed through its thousands of calculations a second. Three months of this, thought George, was enough to start anyone climbing up the wall.

"There she is!" called Chuck, pointing down into the valley. "Ain't she beautiful!"

She certainly was, thought George. The battered old DC3 lay at the end of the runway like a tiny silver cross. In two hours she would be bearing them away to freedom and sanity. It was a thought worth savoring like a fine liqueur. George let it roll round his mind as the pony trudged patiently down the slope.

The swift night of the high Himalayas was now almost upon them. Fortunately, the road was very good, as roads went in that region, and they were both carrying torches. There was not the slightest danger, only a certain discomfort from the bitter cold. The sky overhead was perfectly clear, and ablaze with the familiar, friendly stars. At least there would be no risk, thought George, of the pilot being unable to take off because of weather conditions. That had been his only remaining worry.

He began to sing, but gave it up after a while. This vast arena of mountains, gleaming like whitely hooded ghosts on every side, did not encourage such ebullience. Presently George glanced at his watch.

"Should be there in an hour," he called back over his shoulder to Chuck. Then he added, in an afterthought: "Wonder if the computer's finished its run. It was due about now."

Chuck didn't reply, so George swung round in his saddle. He could just see Chuck's face, a white oval turned toward the sky.

"Look," whispered Chuck, and George lifted his eyes to heaven. (There is always a last time for everything.)

Overhead, without any fuss, the stars were going out.

The Rotifers

ROBERT ABERNATHY

Henry Chatham thought only the best was good enough for his son, Harry. That was why he bought him such an expensive microscope. Harry's mother grumbled at the expense and thought Harry could ruin his eyesight peering into the machine. Because Harry, repaying his father's generosity ten-fold, kept his eyes glued to the eyepiece almost constantly. He had found a perfectly formed world of weird shapes, colors, — and inhabitants. But then that world turned into a menacing one and Harry became ill . . . a very strange illness.

Henry Chatham knelt by his garden pond, a glass fishbowl cupped in his thin, nervous hands. Carefully he dipped the bowl into the green-scummed water and, moving it gently, let trailing streamers of submerged water weeds drift into it. Then he picked up the old scissors he had laid on the bank, and clipped the stems of the floating plants, getting as much of them as he could in the container.

When he righted the bowl and got stiffly to his feet, it contained, he thought hopefully, a fair cross-section of fresh-water plankton. He was pleased with himself for remembering that term from the book he had studied assiduously for the last few nights in order to be able to cope with Harry's inevitable questions.

There was even a shiny black water beetle doing insane circles on the surface of the water. At sight of the insect, the eyes of the twelve-year-old boy, who had been standing by in silent expectation, widened with interest.

"What's that thing, Dad?" he asked excitedly. "What's that crazy bug?"

"I don't know its scientific name, I'm afraid," said Henry Chatham. "But when I was a boy we used to call them whirligig beetles."

"He doesn't seem to think he has enough room in the bowl," said Harry thoughtfully. "Maybe we better put him back in the pond, Dad."

"I thought you might want to look at him through the microscope," the father said in some surprise.

"I think we ought to put him back," insisted Harry.

Mr. Chatham held the dripping bowl obligingly. Harry's hand, a thin boy's hand with narrow, sensitive fingers, hovered over the water, and when the beetle paused for a moment in its gyrations, made a dive for it.

But the whirligig beetle saw the hand coming, and, quicker than a wink, plunged under the water and scooted rapidly to the very bottom of the bowl.

Harry's young face was rueful; he wiped his wet hand on his trousers. "I guess he wants to stay," he supposed.

The two went up the garden path together and into the house, Mr. Chatham bearing the fishbowl before him like a votive offering. Harry's mother met them at the door, brandishing an old towel.

"Here," she said firmly, "you wipe that thing off before you bring it in the house. And don't drip any of that dirty pond water on my good carpet."

"It's not dirty," said Henry Chatham. "It's just full of life, plants and animals too small for the eye to see. But Harry's going to see them with his microscope." He accepted the towel and wiped the bowl; then, in the living room, he set it beside an open window, where the summer sun slanted in and fell on the green plants.

The brand-new microscope stood nearby, in a good light. It was an expensive microscope, no toy for a child, and it magnified four hundred diameters. Henry Chatham had bought it because he believed that his only son showed a desire to peer into the mysteries of smallness, and so far Harry had not disappointed him. Together they had compared hairs from their two heads, had seen the point of a fine sewing needle make to look like the tip of a crowbar, had made grains of salt look like chunks of glass brick, had captured a housefly and marveled at its clawed hairy feet, its great red-faceted eyes, and the delicate veining and fringing of its wings.

Now he let Harry find the glass slide with a cup ground into it, and another smooth slip of glass to cover it. Then he half-showed, half-told him how to scrape gently along the bottom sides of the drifting leaves, to capture the teeming life that dwelt there in the slime. When the boy understood, his young hands were quickly more skillful than his father's; they filled the well with a few drops of water that was promisingly green and murky.

Already Harry knew how to adjust the lighting mirror under the stage of the microscope and turn the focusing screws. He did so, bent intently over the eyepiece, squinting down the polished barrel in the happy expectation of wonders.

"Have you got it, Harry?" asked his father after two or three minutes during which the boy did not move.

Harry took a last long look, then glanced up, blinking slightly.

"You look, Dad!" he exclaimed warmly. "It's — it's like a garden in the water, full of funny little people!"

Mr. Chatham bent to gaze into the eyepiece. This was new to him too, and instantly he saw the aptness of Harry's simile. There

was a garden there, of weird, green transparent stalks composed of plainly visible
cells fastened end to end, with globules and
bladders like fruits or seed-pods attached to
them, floating among them; and in the garden
the strange little people swam to and fro, or
clung with odd appendages to the stalks and
branches. Their bodies were transparent like
the plants, and in them were pulsing hearts
and other organs plainly visible. They looked
a little like sea horses with pointed tails, but
their heads were different, small and
rounded, with big, dark, glistening eyes.

All at once Mr. Chatham realized that
Harry was speaking to him, still in high
excitement.

"What are they, Dad?" he begged to know.

His father straightened up and shook his
head. "I don't know, Harry," he answered
slowly, casting about in his memory. He
seemed to remember a microphotograph of a
creature like those in the book he had studied,
but the name that had gone with it eluded
him.

He bent over once more to immerse his
eyes and mind in the green water-garden on
the slide. The little creatures swam to and fro
as before, growing hazy and dwindling or
swelling as they swam out of the narrow focus
of the lens; he gazed at those who paused in
sharp definition, and saw that, although he
had at first seen no visible means of propulsion, each creature bore about its head a halo
of threadlike, flickering cilia that lashed the

water and drew it forward, for all the world like an airplane propeller or a rapidly turning wheel.

"I know what they are!" exclaimed Henry Chatham, turning to his son with an almost boyish excitement. "They're rotifers! That means 'wheel-bearers,' and they were called that because to the first scientists who saw them it looked like they swam with wheels."

Harry had got down the book and was leafing through the pages. He looked up seriously. "Here they are," he said. "Here's a picture that looks almost like the ones in our pond water."

"Let's see," said his father. They looked at the pictures and descriptions of the Rotifera; there was a good deal of concrete information on the habits and physiology of these odd and complex little animals. It said that they were much more highly organized than Protozoa, having a discernible heart, brain, digestive system, and nervous system, and that their reproduction was by means of two sexes like that of the higher orders. Beyond that, they were a mystery; their relationship to other life forms remained shrouded in doubt.

"You've got something interesting here," said Henry Chatham with satisfaction. "Maybe you'll find out something about them that nobody knows yet."

He was pleased when Harry spent all the rest of that Sunday afternoon peering into the microscope, watching the rotifers, and even more pleased when the boy found a pencil and paper and tried, in an amateurish way, to draw and describe what he saw in the green water garden.

Beyond a doubt, Henry thought, here was a hobby that Harry loved.

Mrs. Chatham was not so pleased. When her husband laid down his evening paper and went into the kitchen for a drink of water, she cornered him and hissed at him: "I told you you had no business buying Harry a thing like that! If he keeps on at this rate, he'll wear his eyes out in no time."

Henry Chatham set down his water glass and looked straight at his wife. "Sally, Harry's eyes are young and he's using them to learn with. You've never been much worried over me, using my eyes up eight hours a day, five days a week, over a blind-alley bookkeeping job."

He left her angrily silent and went back to his paper.

Once the boy glanced up from his periodic drawing and asked with the air of one who proposes a pondered question: "Dad, if you look through a microscope the wrong way is it a telescope?"

Mr. Chatham lowered his paper and bit his underlip. "I don't think so — no, I don't know. When you look through a microscope, it makes things seem closer — one way, that is; if you looked the other way, it would probably make them seem farther off. What did you want to know for?"

"Oh — nothing." Harry turned back to his work. As if in afterthought, he explained, "I was wondering if the rotifers could see me when I'm looking at them."

In the following days his interest became more and more intense. He spent long hours, almost without moving, watching the rotifers. For the little animals had become the sole object which he desired to study under the microscope, and even his father found it difficult to understand such an enthusiasm.

During the long hours at the office to which he commuted, Henry Chatham often found the vision of his son, absorbed with the invisible world that the microscope had opened to him, coming between him and the columns in the ledgers. And sometimes, too, he envisioned the dim green water garden where the little things swam to and fro, and a strangeness filled his thoughts.

On Wednesday evening, he glanced at the fishbowl and noticed that the whirligig beetle was missing. Casually, he asked his son about it.

"I had to get rid of him," said the boy with a trace of uneasiness in his manner. "I took him out and squashed him."

"Why did you have to do that?"

"He was eating the rotifers and their eggs," said Harry, with what seemed to be a touch of remembered anger at the beetle.

"How did you find out he was eating them?" inquired Mr. Chatham, feeling a warmth of pride at the thought that Harry had discovered such a scientific fact for himself.

The boy hesitated oddly. "I — I looked it up in the books."

His father masked his faint disappointment. "That's fine," he said. "I guess you find out more about them all the time."

"Uh-huh," admitted Harry, turning back to his table.

There was undoubtedly something a little strange about Harry's manner; and now Mr. Chatham realized that it had been two days since Harry had asked him to "Quick, take a look!" at the newest wonder he had discovered. With this thought teasing at his mind, the father walked casually over to the table where his son sat hunched and, looking down at the litter of slides and papers — some of which were covered with figures and scribblings of which he could make nothing. He said diffidently, "How about a look?"

Harry glanced up as if startled. He was silent a moment; then he slid reluctantly from his chair and said, "All right."

Mr. Chatham sat down and bent over the microscope. Puzzled and a little hurt, he twirled the focusing vernier and peered into the eyepiece, looking down into the green water world of the rotifers.

There was a swarm of them under the lens, and they swam lazily to and fro, their cilia beating like miniature propellers. Their dark eyes stared, wet and glistening; they drifted in the motionless water, and clung with suckerlike pseudo-feet to the tangled plants.

Then, as he almost looked away, one of them detached itself from the group and swam upward, toward him, growing larger and blurring as it rose out of the focus of the microscope. The last thing that remained defined, before it became a shapeless gray blob and vanished, was the dark blotches of the great cold eyes, seeming to stare full at him — cold, motionless, but alive.

Henry Chatham drew suddenly back from the eyepiece, with an involuntary shudder that he could not explain to himself. He said haltingly, "They look interesting."

"Sure, Dad," said Harry. He moved to occupy the chair again, and his dark young head bowed once more over the microscope. His father walked back across the room and sank gratefully into his armchair — after all, it had been a hard day at the office. He watched Harry work the focusing screws, then take his pencil and begin to write quickly and impatiently.

It was with a guilty feeling of prying that, after Harry had been sent reluctantly to bed, Henry Chatham took a tentative look at those papers which lay on his son's worktable. He frowned uncomprehendingly at the things that were written there; it was neither mathematics nor language, but many of the scribblings were jumbles of letters and figures. It looked like code, and he remembered that less than a year ago, Harry had been passionately interested in cryptography. But what did cryptography have to do with microscopy, or codes with — rotifers?

Nowhere did there seem to be a key, but there were occasional words and phrases jotted into the margins of some of the sheets. Mr. Chatham read these, and learned nothing. "Can't dry up, but they can," said one. "Beds of germs," said another. And in the corner of one sheet, "1 — Yes. 2 — No." The only thing that looked like a translation was the note: "rty34pr is the pond."

Mr. Chatham shook his head bewilderedly. Why should Harry want to keep notes on his scientific hobby in code? He went to bed still puzzling, but it did not keep him from sleeping, for he was tired.

Then, only the next evening, his wife maneuvered to get him alone with her and burst out passionately:

"Henry, I told you that microscope was going to ruin Harry's eyesight! I was watching him today when he didn't know I was watching him, and I saw him winking and blinking right while he kept on looking into the thing. I was minded to stop him then and there, but I want you to assert your authority with him and tell him he can't go on."

"All right, Sally," said Mr. Chatham wearily. "I'll see if I can't persuade him to be a little more moderate."

He went slowly into the living room. At the moment, Harry was not using the microscope; instead, he seemed to be studying one of his cryptic pages of notes. As his father entered, he looked up sharply and swiftly laid the sheet down — face down.

Perhaps it wasn't all Sally's imagination; the boy did look nervous, and there was a drawn, white look to his thin young face. His father said gently, "Harry, Mother tells me she saw you blinking, as if your eyes were tired, when you were looking into the microscope today. You know if you look too much, it can be a strain on your sight."

Harry nodded quickly, too quickly, perhaps. "Yes, Dad," he said. "I read that in the book. It says there that if you close the eye you're looking with for a little while, it rests you and your eyes don't get tired. So I was practicing that this afternoon. Mother must have been watching me then, and got the wrong idea."

"Oh," said Henry Chatham. "Well, it's good that you're trying to be careful. But you've got your mother worried, and that's not so good. I wish, myself, that you wouldn't spend all your time with the microscope. Don't you ever play baseball with the fellows any more?"

"I haven't got time," said the boy, with a curious stubborn twist to his mouth. "I can't right now, Dad."

"Your rotifers won't die if you leave them alone for a while. And if they do, there'll always be a new crop."

"But I'd lose track of them," said Harry strangely. "Their lives are so short — they live so awfully fast. You don't know how fast they live."

"I've seen them," answered his father. "I

guess they're fast, all right." He did not know quite what to make of it all, so he settled himself in his chair with his paper.

But that night, after Harry had gone to bed, he stirred himself to take down the book that dealt with life in pond-water. There was a memory pricking at his mind; the memory of the water beetle, which Harry had killed because, he said, he was eating the rotifers and their eggs.

Mr. Chatham turned through the book; he read, with aching eyes, all that it said about rotifers. He searched for information on the beetle, and found there was a whole family of whirligig beetles. There was some material here on the characteristics and habits of the Gyrinidae, but nowhere did it mention the devouring of rotifers or their eggs among their customs.

Harry must have lied. But why in God's name should he say he'd looked a thing up in the book when he must have found it out for himself, the hard way?

Henry Chatham slept badly that night and dreamed distorted dreams. But when the alarm clock shrilled, jarring him awake, the dream in which he had been immersed skittered away to the back of his mind.

During the morning his work went slowly, for he kept pausing, sometimes in the midst of totaling a column of figures, to grasp at some mocking half-memory of that dream. At last, elbows on his desk, staring unseeingly at the clock on the wall, his mind went back to Harry, dark head bowed motionless over the barrel of his microscope, looking, always looking into the pale green water gardens and the unseen lives of the beings that . . .

All at once it came to him, the dream he had dreamed. *He* had been bending over the microscope, *he* had been looking into the unseen world, and the horror of what he had seen gripped him now and brought out the chill sweat on his body.

For he had seen his son there in the clouded water, among the twisted grassy plants, his face turned upward and eyes wide in the agonized appeal of the drowning; around him had been a swarm of the weird creatures, and they had been dragging him down, blurring out of focus, and their great dark eyes glistening wetly, coldly. . . .

He was sitting rigid at his desk, his work forgotten; all at once he saw the clock and noticed with a start that it was already eleven A.M. A fear he could not define seized him, and his hand reached spasmodically for the telephone on his desk.

But before he touched it, it began ringing.

After a moment's paralysis, he picked up the receiver. It was his wife's voice that came shrilly over the wires.

"Henry, you've got to come home right now. Harry's sick. He's got a high fever, and he's been asking for you."

He moistened his lips and said, "I'll be right home. I'll take a taxi."

"Hurry!" she exclaimed. "He's been saying queer things. I think he's delirious." She paused, and added, "And it's all the fault of that microscope you bought him!"

"I'll be right home," he repeated dully.

His wife was not at the door to meet him. He paused in the living room and glanced toward the table that bore the microscope; the black, gleaming thing still stood there, but he did not see any of the slides, and the papers were piled neatly together to one side. His eyes fell on the fishbowl; it was empty, clean and shining. He knew Harry hadn't done those things; that was Sally's neatness.

Abruptly, instead of going straight up the stairs, he moved to the table and looked down at the pile of papers. The one on top was almost blank; on it was written several times: rty34pr . . . rty34pr . . . His memory for figure combinations served him; he remembered what had been written on another page: "rty34pr is the pond."

A step on the stairs jerked him around.

It was his wife, of course. She said in a voice sharp-edged with apprehension: "What are you doing down here? Harry wants you. The doctor hasn't come; I phoned him just before I called you, but he hasn't come."

He did not answer. Instead he gestured at the pile of papers, the empty fishbowl, an imperative question on his face.

"I threw that dirty water back in the pond. It's probably what he caught something from.

And he was breaking himself down, humping over that thing. It's your fault, for getting it. Are you coming?"

"I'm coming," he said heavily, and followed her upstairs.

Harry lay back in his bed. His head was propped against a single pillow, and his eyes were half-closed, the lids swollen looking, his face hotly flushed. He was breathing slowly as if asleep.

But as his father entered the room, he opened his eyes as if with an effort, fixed them on him, said, "Dad . . . I've got to tell you."

Mr. Chatham took the chair by the bedside, quietly. He asked, "About what, Harry?"

The boy's eyes shifted to his mother, at the foot of his bed. "I don't want to talk to her. *She* thinks it's just fever. But you'll understand."

Henry Chatham lifted his gaze to meet his wife's. "Maybe you'd better go downstairs and wait for the doctor, Sally."

She looked hard at him, then turned abruptly and closed the door softly behind her.

"Now what did you want to tell me, Harry?"

"About *them* . . . the rotifers," the boy said. His eyes had drifted half-shut again, but his voice was clear. "They did it to me. . . ."

"Did *what*?"

"I don't know. . . . They used one of their cultures. They've got all kinds: beds of germs, under the leaves in the water. They've been growing new kinds, that will be worse than

anything that ever was before. . . . They live
so fast, they work so fast.

"It was only a little while, before I found
out they knew about me. I could see them
through my microscope, but they could see
me, too. . . . They know about us, now, and
they hate us. They never knew before — that
there was anybody but them. . . . So they want
to kill us all."

"But why should they want to do that?"
asked the father, gently.

"They don't like knowing that they aren't
the only ones on Earth that can think. I expect
people would be the same way."

"But they're such little things, Harry. They
can't hurt us at all."

The boy's eyes opened wide, shadowed with
terror and fever. "I told you, Dad — They're
growing germs, millions and billions of them,
new ones. . . . And they kept telling me to
take them back to the pond, so they could
tell all the rest, and they could all start getting
ready — for war."

He remembered the shapes that swam and
crept in the green water gardens, with whirling
cilia and great, cold, glistening eyes. And he
remembered the clean, empty fishbowl in the
window downstairs.

"Don't let them, Dad," said Harry convulsively. "You've got to kill them all. The ones
here and the ones in the pond. You've got to
kill them good — because they don't mind being killed, and they lay lots of eggs, and their
eggs can stand almost anything, even drying

up. And the eggs remember what the old ones knew."

"Don't worry," said Henry Chatham quickly. He grasped his son's hand, a hot, limp hand that had slipped from under the coverlet. "We'll stop them. We'll drain the pond."

"I ought to have told you before, Dad — but first I was afraid you'd laugh, and then — I was just . . . afraid. . . ."

His voice drifted away. And his father, looking down at the flushed face, saw that he seemed asleep. Well, that was better than the sick delirium — saying such strange, wild things —

Downstairs the doctor was saying harshly, "All right. But let's have a look at the patient."

Henry Chatham came quietly downstairs; he greeted the doctor briefly, and did not follow him to Harry's bedroom.

When he was left alone in the room, he went to the window and stood looking down at the microscope. He could not rid his head of strangeness: A window between two worlds, our world and that of the infinitely small, a window that looks both ways.

After a time, he went through the kitchen and let himself out the back door, into the noonday sunlight.

He followed the garden path until he came to the edge of the little pond. It lay there quiet in the sunlight, green-scummed, and walled with stiff rank grass, a lone dragonfly swooping and wheeling above it. The image of all the stagnant waters, the fertile breeding-places of strange life, with which it was joined in the end by the tortuous hidden channels, the oozing pores of the Earth.

And it seemed to him then that he glimpsed something, a hitherto unseen miasma, rising above the pool and darkening the sunlight ever so little. A dream, a shadow — the shadow of the alien dream of things hidden in smallness, the dark dream of the rotifers.

Henry Chatham was suddenly afraid. He turned and walked slowly, wearily, up the path toward the house.

Does a Bee Care?

ISAAC ASIMOV

Hammer had noticed him from the beginning of the project. There was something odd about the way Kane went about his work building the space craft. He had a faraway look in his eyes, as though he was searching for something he couldn't quite find. What was it about Kane that seemed so remote, so alien?

The ship began as a metal skeleton. Slowly a shining skin was layered on without and odd-shaped vitals were crammed within.

Thornton Hammer, of all the individuals (but one) involved in the growth, did the least physically. Perhaps that was why he was most highly regarded. He handled the mathematical symbols that formed the basis for lines on drafting paper, which, in turn, formed the basis for the fitting together of the various masses and different forms of energy that went into the ship.

Hammer watched now through close-fitting spectacles somberly. Their lenses caught the light of the fluorescent tubes above and sent them out again as highlights. Theodore Lengyel, representing Personnel of the corporation that was footing the bill for the project, stood beside him and said, as he pointed with a rigid, stabbing finger:

"There he is. That's the man."

Hammer peered. "You mean Kane?"

"The fellow in the green overalls, holding a wrench."

"That's Kane. Now what is this you've got against him?"

"I want to know what he does. The man's an idiot." Lengyel had a round, plump face and his jowls quivered a bit.

Hammer turned to look at the other, his spare body assuming an air of displeasure along every inch. "Have you been bothering him?"

"*Bothering* him? I've been talking to him. It's my job to talk to the men, to get their viewpoints, to get information out of which I can build campaigns for improved morale."

"How does Kane disturb that?"

"He's insolent. I asked him how it felt to be working on a ship that would reach the moon. I talked a little about the ship being a pathway to the stars. Perhaps I made a little speech about it, built it up a bit, when he turned away in the rudest possible manner. I called him back and said, 'Where are you going?' And he said, 'I get tired of that kind of talk. I'm going out to look at the stars.' "

Hammer nodded. "All right. Kane likes to look at the stars."

"It was daytime. The man's an idiot. I've been watching him since and he doesn't do any work."

"I know that."

"Then why is he kept on?"

Hammer said with a sudden, tight fierceness, "Because I want him around. Because he's my luck."

"Your luck?" faltered Lengyel. "What the hell does that mean?"

"It means that when he's around I think better. When he passes me, holding his damned wrench, I get ideas. It's happened three times. I don't explain it; I'm not interested in explaining it. It's happened. He stays."

"You're joking."

"No, I'm not. Now leave me alone."

Kane stood there in his green overalls, holding his wrench.

Dimly he was aware that the ship was almost ready. It was not designed to carry a man, but there was space for a man. He knew that the way he knew a lot of things; like keeping out of the way of most people most of the time; like carrying a wrench until people grew used to him carrying a wrench and stopped noticing it. Protective coloration consisted of little things, really — like carrying the wrench.

He was full of drives he did not fully understand, like looking at the stars. At first, many years back, he had just looked at the stars with a vague ache. Then, slowly, his attention centered itself on a certain region of the sky, then to a certain pinpointed spot. He didn't know why that certain spot. There were no stars in that spot. There was nothing to see.

That spot was high in the night sky in the late spring and in the summer months, and he sometimes spent most of the night watching the spot until it sank toward the southwestern horizon. At other times in the year he would stare at the spot during the day.

There was some thought in connection with that spot which he couldn't quite crystallize. It had grown stronger, come nearer to the surface as the years passed, and it was almost bursting for expression now. But still it had not quite come clear.

Kane shifted restlessly and approached the ship. It was almost complete, almost whole. Everything fitted just so. Almost.

For within it, far forward, was a hole a little larger than a man; and leading to that hole was a pathway a little wider than a man. Tomorrow that pathway would be filled with the last of the vitals, and before that was done the hole had to be filled, too. But not with anything *they* planned.

Kane moved still closer and no one paid

any attention to him. They were used to him.

There was a metal ladder that had to be climbed and a catwalk that had to be moved along to enter the last opening. He knew where the opening was as exactly as if he had built the ship with his own hands. He climbed the ladder and moved along the catwalk. There was no one there at the mo —

He was wrong. One man.

That one said sharply, "What are you doing here?"

Kane straightened and his vague eyes stared at the speaker. He lifted his wrench and brought it down on the speaker's head lightly. The man who was struck (and who had made no effort to ward off the blow) dropped, partly from the effect of the blow.

Kane let him lie there, without concern. The man would not remain unconscious for long, but long enough to allow Kane to wriggle into the hole. When the man revived he would recall nothing about Kane or about the fact of his own unconsciousness. There would simply be five minutes taken out of his life that he would never find and never miss.

It was dark in the hole and, of course, there was no ventilation, but Kane paid no attention to that. With the sureness of instinct, he clambered upward toward the hold that would receive him, then lay there, panting, fitting the cavity neatly, as though it were a womb.

In two hours they would begin inserting the last of the vitals, close the passage, and leave Kane there, unknowingly. Kane would be the sole bit of flesh and blood in a thing of metal and ceramics and fuel.

Kane was not afraid of being prematurely discovered. No one in the project knew the hole was there. The design didn't call for it. The mechanics and construction men weren't aware of having put it in.

Kane had arranged that entirely by himself.

He didn't know how he had arranged it but he knew he had.

He could watch his own influence without knowing how it was exerted. Take the man Hammer, for instance, the leader of the project and the most clearly influenced. Of all the indistinct figures about Kane, he was the least indistinct. Kane would be very aware of him at times, when he passed near him in his slow and hazy journeys about the grounds. It was all that was necessary — passing near him.

Kane recalled it had been so before, particularly with theoreticians. When Lise Meitner decided to test for barium among the products of the neutron bombardment of uranium, Kane had been there, an unnoticed plodder along a corridor nearby.

He had been picking up leaves and trash in a park in 1904 when the young Einstein had passed by, pondering. Einstein's steps had quickened with the impact of sudden thought. Kane felt it like an electric shock.

But he didn't know how it was done. Does a spider know architectural theory when it begins to construct its first web?

It went further back. The day the young

Newton had stared at the moon with the dawn of a certain thought, Kane had been there. And further back still.

The panorama of New Mexico, ordinarily deserted, was alive with human ants crawling about the metal shaft lancing upward. This one was different from all the similar structures that had preceded it.

This would go free of Earth more nearly than any other. It would reach out and circle the moon before falling back. It would be crammed with instruments that would photograph the moon and measure its heat emissions, probe for radioactivity, and test by microwave for chemical structure. It would, by automation, do almost everything that could be expected of a manned vehicle. And it would learn enough to make certain that the next ship sent out *would* be a manned vehicle.

Except that, in a way, this first one was a manned vehicle after all.

There were representatives of various governments, of various industries, of various social and economic groupings. There were television cameras and feature writers.

Those who could not be there watched in their homes and heard numbers counted backward in painstaking monotone in the manner grown traditional in a mere three decades.

At zero the reaction motors came to life and ponderously the ship lifted.

* * *

Kane heard the noise of the rushing gases, as though from a distance, and felt the gathering acceleration press against him.

He detached his mind, lifting it up and outward, freeing it from direct connection with his body in order that he might be unaware of the pain and discomfort.

Dizzily, he knew his long journey was nearly over. He would no longer have to maneuver carefully to avoid having people realize he was immortal. He would no longer have to fade into the background, no longer wander eternally from place to place, changing names and personality, manipulating minds.

It had not been perfect, of course. The myths of the Wandering Jew and the Flying Dutchman had arisen, but he was still here. He had not been disturbed.

He could see his spot in the sky. Through the mass and solidity of the ship he could see it. Or not "see" really. He didn't have the proper word.

He knew there was a proper word, though. He could not say how he knew a fraction of the things he knew, except that as the centuries had passed he had gradually grown to know them with a sureness that required no reason.

He had begun as an ovum (or as something for which "ovum" was the nearest word he knew), deposited on Earth before the first cities had been built by the wandering hunting creatures since called "men." Earth had been chosen carefully by his progenitor. Not every world would do.

What world would? What was the criterion? That he still didn't know.

Does an ichneumon wasp study ornithology before it finds the one species of spider that will do for her eggs, and stings it just so in order that it may remain alive?

The ovum spilt him forth at length and he took the shape of a man and lived among men and protected himself against men. And his one purpose was to arrange to have men travel along a path that would end with a ship and within the ship a hole and within the hole, himself.

It had taken eight thousand years of slow striving and stumbling.

The spot in the sky became sharper now as the ship moved out of the atmosphere. That was the key that opened his mind. That was the piece that completed the puzzle.

Stars blinked within that spot that could not be seen by a man's eye unaided. One in particular shone brilliantly and Kane yearned toward it. The expression that had been building within him for so long burst out now.

"Home," he whispered.

He knew? Does a salmon study cartography to find the headwaters of the fresh-water stream in which years before it had been born?

The final step was taken in the slow maturing that had taken eight thousand years, and Kane was no longer larval, but adult.

The adult Kane fled from the human flesh that had protected the larva, and fled the ship, too. It hastened onward, at inconceivable speeds, toward home, from which someday it, too, might set off on wanderings through space to fertilize some planet with its ovum.

It sped through Space, giving no thought to the ship carrying an empty chrysalis. It gave no thought to the fact that it had driven a whole world toward technology and space travel in order only that the thing that had been Kane might mature and reach its fulfillment.

Does a bee care what has happened to a flower when the bee has done and gone its way?